RED FLAGGED

RECLAIMED HEARTS
BOOK 3

ELLE KEATON

DIRTY DOG
PRESS

WHO'S WHO IN THE COOPER SPRINGS UNIVERSE

If this is your very first Reclaimed Hearts book this list will help you figure out who is who. If you are old, like me, it will REMIND you who is who—and what book they appeared in.

Xavier Stone - Main character from Adverse Conditions. Real estate agent. Has a twin brother named Max (his story is in Mandatory Repairs)

Vincent Barone - Xavier's (now) boyfriend. High school shop teacher and all-around good guy. Except when it comes to Xavier.

Romy - Vincent's high school age daughter.

Kimball Frye - Owner of West Coast Forensics, he and Devon Flynn get their story in Real Risk.

Rufus Ferguson - Magnus Ferguson's father, used to own the Steam Donkey, president of the local Big Foot Society.

Magnus Ferguson - Rufus's son, owner of the Steam Donkey, Shakespearean Actor and producer.

Lani Cooper - Cooper Springs Police deputy.

Forrest Cooper - Lani's older brother and Xavier's best friend.

Nick Waugh - He and Martin Purdy get together in **Below Grade.**

Sasha Bolic - A former US Marshal who first appears in No Pressure from Shielded Hearts and gets his story in As Sure as the Sun.

Niall Hamarsson - Ex-homicide detective, now works for West Coast Forensics. Appears first in Conspiracy Theory (Veiled Intentions).

Ethan Moore - Forensic Anthropologist. We meet him briefly in Black Moon (Veiled Intentions).

Lizzy Harlow - appears in **Adverse Conditions.**

Jayden and Abby Harlow - Lizzy's two children.

RAVEN

Raven circled over the beach in wide, swooping movements. It was easy to spot the two dark figures far below. Rain and wind buffeted her, but she didn't care. Wind, rain, heat, it all was the way of life. If anything, the gusts made things just a little more exciting.

When the first man stepped onto the beach, the other hesitated before following him.

They trudged across the wet sand a short distance before stopping near a careless pile of driftwood and sitting shoulder to shoulder on a battered tree trunk. That one had left the forest long ago; Raven knew it didn't mind.

A few yards away from the men, two gray and white seagulls huddled against the sand, a safe distance from the waves. Their tail feathers fluttered as the wind gusted around them. A lone cormorant that had claimed a channel marker for its own spread its wings wide, as if that would dry them in this weather. If she could have, Raven would have rolled her eyes. Instead, she released her version of a scoff and kept her eye on the humans.

The wind died down for a moment and Raven let herself soar downward, landing on a log not far from where the men sat. She was curious by nature, but it wasn't pure curiosity that brought her here today.

"She's gone. I know she's gone. I can feel it," said one of the men as he stared, unseeing, out toward the crashing waves and the limitless horizon.

"You don't know that," replied the other one. He scooted close and put his arm around the first man's shoulders.

Raven hopped closer, cocking her head to the side. As much as was possible for her, she felt something close to remorse. A certain pinch that meant sadness. Some secrets had to stay secret. There was an order that needed to be followed. A secret exposed too soon meant another could be passed by, unseen and unnoticed. The ancient ones had put things in motion and their secret was paramount, only just beginning to be revealed.

One didn't trust humans to stay on task. They were easily distracted at the best of times. Still, the desire to communicate with the sad man niggled at her. He was so clearly in anguish. Grief was an emotion Raven understood. She wished she could tell him that nothing was his fault. The evil was deep and entrenched. It had gone too long without check and so the great ones had decided to act.

The sad man's shoulders began to heave. Raven could see his spirit leaving his body. Not dying, no, not that, but a fading of his light, as if this tragedy was too much for him. She wanted to assure him he would get through this time, but he wouldn't listen. He wouldn't hear her.

The storm strengthened and the clouds regained their momentum, again racing toward the shore where the two men huddled and Raven eavesdropped. Eventually, with a flap of her wings and a caw, she lifted off toward the shelter of the forest, letting the wind do most of the work for her.

Below her, the human settlement was quiet. This was not the time when humans were outside in abundance.

This was the secret season.

ONE

André's evening reading was interrupted by a banging against his front door. The hammering was loud, purposeful, and, in André's opinion, full of false promise. He briefly contemplated not answering. The reverberation alone told him who was on the other side.

He had a choice to make.

For fuck's sake, the thundering knock hadn't even startled him.

Damn.

Annoyed, he set his mystery novel—a British cozy he'd been half paying attention to while listening to the rain pound against the roof—face down on the arm of the couch and rose to his feet. Traitorous anticipation bloomed slowly, languorously, alongside the growing exasperation in the pit of his stomach, rising like the steam from a freshly brewed cup of tea.

"Dear, I know you're in there. Answer the fucking door. It's pissing down out here."

Wasn't forty-five too old for a booty call? Was it a booty call when the ass in question showed up unannounced and, well, *uncalled?*

André didn't have time to answer any of that in the short distance between his couch and the front door. Reaching out, he flipped the lock open and then twisted the handle, his hand shaking slightly.

This would be the last time.

Seconds later, André was slammed back against the living room wall, his hands automatically slipping under Dante's leather jacket and cotton t-shirt, his fingertips sliding against Dante's chilled, damp, skin. Dante murmured something and then his mouth was on André's, claiming him as he always did.

Always. But never forever.

Within minutes, they were mostly naked and stumbling into André's bedroom. A trail of clothing was strewn behind them, much like Hansel and Gretel's trail of breadcrumbs so they could find their way back out of the wicked forest.

André felt his personal forest was much more complicated than Hansel and Gretel's, but he'd finally found a way out of it.

This was the last time they were doing this.

At least this time, they made it to the bed and hadn't just ended up on the couch like so many nights before. Falling onto the mattress, André had landed on his back and currently was gazing down his body, watching an equally naked Dante press his nose into André's crotch. He liked it.

God, he liked it.

His cock did too. His cock was a fan of *everything* Dante. But it needed to stop. It had to. A relationship that consisted of late-night knocks on the door (followed up by the best sex André had ever experienced) and an empty spot next to him in the morning was not what he wanted.

The sex was incredible but what happened afterward made him intensely lonely.

As ridiculous as it was for a man of his age and profession—a

U.S. Marshal, for godsakes—André wanted a partner. A real partner.

Dante Castone, an undercover operator for the DEA, was not the man for the job.

He wanted someone who'd stand by his side through good and bad times and vice versa. Dante was not that man. No matter how fucking incredible his lips felt as they closed around André's cock.

"Jesus," André groaned, arching his back.

Since a partner didn't seem to be in the cards for André at this late stage in the game, he'd decided to settle for a job that wasn't actively trying to kill him. He wanted to head into his twilight years like a cop on *The Andy Griffith Show* or *Mayberry R.F.D.*, giving advice to innocent kids and chatting with senior citizens who would end up having the answer to everything.

"You're distracted tonight," Dante rumbled as he let André's cock slip from between his lips so he could begin licking his way up André's body. He was heading toward André's neck, which seemed to be a favorite place of his.

"Don't leave marks," André complained, his hips jerking as Dante nibbled on a sensitive nipple. "I don't want to have to explain anything to my coworkers."

"So many rules. You know I love breaking rules."

Dante did love breaking rules—André's rules, at any rate.

"Quit thinking so hard." Dante punctuated his demand by biting and then sucking hard on André's nipple, tracing around the nub with his hot tongue.

"Fuck." André's cock throbbed with anticipation of what was to come—himself and Dante—and he writhed desperately underneath Dante's pleasantly heavy, muscular body, needing more contact, more of everything.

Tomorrow he'd tell Dante they couldn't do this anymore. No more rule breaking.

. . .

Sometime later, André felt the mattress move underneath him as Dante rolled out of bed. He heard him pad down the hallway to the bathroom. He heard the toilet flush. And then he didn't hear any more.

It had been a long, stressful week—hell, a long, stressful year. A major case he'd been dedicated to had finally broken wide open after over twelve months of hard work. Aldo Campos was in federal custody and the human trafficking and drug distribution ring Aldo had run with his younger brother Alonso was in the midst of being dismantled. André had been on the multi-agency team that brought him in, and now he deserved a good night's rest.

Shutting his eyes, André slid back under the blissful blanket of slumber.

When André woke for the second time, he immediately sensed that Dante was no longer in his house. Had he left at oh-dark thirty? Or had he come back to bed for a little while? They didn't have rules about that—even if Dante teased André about having too many.

Rarely did Dante stay—if leaving before sunrise but after the bars closed could be considered staying. More often he left. Today he was gone. The only steady rule was that André never went to Dante's home. He didn't even know where in Portland the man lived. Maybe he lived in Salem or Gresham? Maybe he had a family he returned to each night?

That thought chilled André to the core.

Wiping the sleep from his eyes, he stumbled to the bathroom, twisting the knobs until the shower came on. Freezing cold water was finally followed by hot, almost instantly steaming up the mirror and window. Maybe his next bathroom would have a fan.

Once he was clean and dressed for the day, and caffeine was making its way into his bloodstream, André opened his laptop to check his email. He'd put it off until he was fully awake and prepared for whatever might be lurking for him there.

The topmost email was what he'd been waiting for. Hoping for. He clicked into it and skimmed the words. Then he reread them slowly, making sure he wasn't misunderstanding anything.

"Yes," he said with a pump of his fist.

This email was his ticket out of the stress of the U.S. Marshals Service and quite possibly an early funeral. A byproduct of the email would be no longer being available for Dante Castone whenever the guy felt like he needed a clandestine fuck.

André had some self-respect left.

Beads of sweat broke out on his brow as he first hit Reply, then typed his response with shaky fingers. YES. Then he pressed the Send button. Without missing a beat, André pulled up the email address for his direct supervisor in downtown Portland, typed out a second email, and sent that one too. When that was finished, he leaned back in his chair, feeling lighter than he had in years.

"Cooper Springs Chief of Police" had a nice ring to it. He'd be starting in just two weeks.

~

"Dear, you fucking asshole." Smitty pounded him on the back with one massive hand. "I can't believe you're leaving the team. We all thought you were a lifer."

Coughing as he tried to reclaim some of the air Smitty had forced out of his lungs, André could do nothing more than wheeze and shake his head.

"Don't kill the guy before he starts his new job," Jensen admonished. "Besides, he'll be back. He's gonna get bored ticketing kids for speeding down Main Street and responding to calls about loose horses."

Frowning, André sucked in a breath as he eyed Jensen, a DEA agent he'd been partnered with to run down Aldo Campos. "I don't think the Olympic Peninsula is exactly horse country."

"Fine." Jensen waved the hand that wasn't wrapped around a full pint of Guinness. "Chickens or"—he guffawed loudly—"Bigfoot."

Little did Jensen know there actually was a Bigfoot Society headquarters in Cooper Springs. And no way was André telling him. Jensen was a fine person, but André wasn't going to miss him. He was loud and brash and generally rubbed André the wrong way. But they'd nabbed Campos together, a feather in both their caps. One worth celebrating.

"It's just not gonna be the same without you," Sacha Bolic said with a false pained air.

"You've been retired for years," André pointed out. "You live in Skagit. Why are you even here tonight?"

André liked Sacha Bolic. He'd been an excellent marshal before hanging up his star and settling down a few years ago. When he'd walked into Kenton Arms, André had done a double take, not remotely expecting to see his former colleague.

"Keeping my hand in," Sacha replied with his trademark evil smirk. Knowing his history, Sacha could have gone either way—good or evil— and André was glad he'd chosen to join the Marshals Service. "Besides, when Doug told me there was a going-away party for your sad ass, Seth and I were already on our way down here for some garden show he can't miss. This way I can catch up with you fools and Seth doesn't have me asking when we can go back to the hotel already."

Seriously, of all the grouchy men on the planet, *Sacha Bolic* had a partner, but André didn't? How was that fair? Even worse, Seth was a nice guy. Younger than Sacha, but a truly nice person who —for some reason—thought Sacha hung the moon and stars.

Searing blue eyes and skin several shades darker than his flickered at the edge of his thoughts. Dante Castone. André figured Dante would hear through the grapevine that André was retiring —had already retired—and was leaving the area. Cops were the biggest fucking gossips on the planet.

It was best this way, André told himself, not for the first time. A clean break. It wasn't as if he and Dante had a real relationship. Even if he'd known how to get in touch with Dante, there was no reason for him to explain anything. André was just wrapping up loose ends on the Campos files and heading into the wild blue yonder. He'd have to testify at the trial when the time came, but other than that? He was done.

"So." Sacha poked him in the ribs, but his tone was serious. What was it with people invading his personal space tonight? "Are you ready for the small-town life?"

Was he ever. André was looking forward to warm coffee and sleeping in his own bed on a regular basis. No more stakeouts in uncomfortable cars. No more chasing fugitives down dark alleys. He could hardly wait.

"I'm as ready as I'll ever be. Definitely looking forward to a slower pace."

Sacha nodded slowly, an irritating *knowing* expression on his face. Like he knew a secret André didn't. "Slower pace, huh? Did you grow up in a small town?"

Thankfully, the rest of the table's attention was diverted by the crackle of the microphone as quiz night started.

"Not so much, and not tiny. Not as small as Cooper Springs."

"Ah," Sacha said, continuing to employ the same irritating tone, his Bosnian accent making an appearance. "So you have no fucking idea what you're getting into?"

Did he? Was he getting in over his own head? André didn't think so. His father had been a police sergeant in the mid-sized town where André had grown up. He was familiar with the vibe, even if it wasn't exactly the same.

"Dear, help me out." Jensen banged him on the shoulder, saving him from having to answer Bolic. "What year did the Beatles break up?"

André glared at the younger man. "Why the hell should I know? I wasn't even born when the Beatles were playing."

"Ah-hah! When were you born? I'll guess a year before that."

Many hours later, André said goodbye to his teammates and coworkers for the last time and slowly walked back to his apartment. A new beginning beckoned him, and he couldn't wait to get started.

TWO

Dante – August

Dante's eyebrows drew together as he scowled at the three words. The text had arrived seconds ago, interrupting what was supposed to be his lunch. His peaceful thirty minutes away from the Iron Joker Outlaw MC gang he'd been working to infiltrate, part of an undercover operation co-run by the DEA and ATF.

A man could only stand so much moral filth in a day. He deserved a break.

H: Check in STAT.

His heart thumped.

It wasn't check-in time—or even check-in day. Dante was undercover in this backwater corner of central Oregon. He set the rules about when to check in with the brass. On the other hand, maybe someone else had found hard evidence proving the club president had first trafficked and then tortured and murdered seventeen-year-old Glory Henderson. There were enough alphabets hanging around the area to make several cans of soup. *Maybe* they'd finally gotten the MC for both arms and human trafficking. That would be an early birthday present.

Something told Dante that wasn't what this text was about. And besides, he'd never gotten what he wanted for his birthday; there was no reason to think the future would be different from the past.

Catching the eye of the lone server, he gestured for her to come back over to his table.

"I'm gonna have to cancel my order," he said, pulling out his wallet and handing a pair of tens over.

"We can box it up for you," she offered.

His phone vibrated again, sending another fission of worry up his spine. Hatch never broke protocol. His handler was nothing if not consistent—and a stickler for rules. Dante met the young woman's dark eyes and shook his head regretfully. This hole-in-the-wall café in the middle of nowhere central Oregon served the best Phad Kee Mao he'd ever eaten.

"That's okay. Thanks for the offer."

Shrugging into his leather jacket, Dante returned his wallet to his back pocket and strode out of the restaurant into the dusty parking lot where the crappy, department-issued, unmarked 1997 Toyota Celica with a manual transmission waited for him. Looks were deceiving though, because under the hood was a refurbished six-cylinder engine that Dante knew from experience could easily cruise at 100 mph. It never hurt to have a means of escape even if he generally stuck to the speed limits.

He waited until the town of Hampton had disappeared from his rearview mirror before pulling over to the side of the road and responding to the text.

D: Checking in

H: Get back to Portland

D: Why

Dante watched the gray dots go back and forth in the chat bubble. Whatever it was, it must be bad. Had the investigation been compromised? Dante hadn't felt like things were falling apart and he was usually able to tell. The unfortunate result of growing up in a toxic household meant he was hyperaware of the people around him.

His phone rang, the sound loud in the confines of the Celica.

"Shit," he murmured. With trepidation unfurling in his stomach, he pressed Accept.

"Castone here."

"Dante." Hatch's voice sounded odd.

"Yeah?"

"It's your sister."

Shit. "Was she in an accident or something?" Simone drove like a Formula 1 driver. Dante hated being in the car with her.

"No. Dante—"

Abruptly, he knew the news was bad. Whatever had happened, it was far worse than a car accident.

"Get to the point. Fucking tell me already."

There was a long silence at the other end of the connection. Every second it took for Hatch to speak had Dante's heart clenching hard, then harder.

"Simone is dead, Dante. Murdered. Last night." Hatch's voice was raspy and broke on the last word.

Dante's chest hurt. He sucked in a gulp of oxygen. Simone and her daughter were the only people in his immediate family Dante had a relationship with—if his other brothers and sisters were even still alive. The Italian Mob may not have been in the news much in the last couple of decades, but they still were around, taking up space on the planet that should have been reserved for good and decent humans.

One of the best people he knew was dead? Gone forever?

"Why? How?" he managed to ask around the bubble of pain in his throat.

"Look, Dante, just come in. You can't go back under—that part of your life is over now. Daniella needs you. She was in the house when it happened."

Shit.

Dante refused to let his brain drag him down the dark path of what his niece might have experienced.

As if reading his mind, Hatch added, "Daniella saw the whole thing. She thinks she might be able to ID one of them when we bring them in."

That was Hatch, always confident. They'd worked together a long time, and Hatch knew how Dante's mind worked.

The fact that Daniella possibly could ID the sons of bitches, that was good. Simone would get justice, then. The fact that Daniella had seen low-life scum end her mother's life was something Dante couldn't get his head around.

"Who did it?"

Another silence before Hatch replied.

"Please, just come in so we can talk in person."

Dante had never heard that tone in Hatch's voice before, and it almost broke him. But he couldn't break, he had to be strong for Dani.

"Who. Fucking. Did. It."

He wracked his brain trying to recall what cases Simone had been working on. As a federal prosecutor, she always had more than one on her plate. Some cases were bigger and more dangerous than others.

"Campos, we think. At least, that he originated the idea." Aldo Campos was currently behind bars waiting for his trial. Dante thought Simone had said they had a court date for September. "But we don't know for sure. Get your ass back to Portland. Your niece needs you."

Dante should've figured it out on his own that the psychopaths who'd murdered his sister would disappear into the ether. No trace, not even sightings at gas stations. They had vanished.

After breaking speeding records his sister would have been

proud of, Dante had arrived at headquarters in North Portland, a run-down strip mall that had once housed a discount shoe store, a nail salon, and a passport photo business. Hatch had hurried him into his office and shut the door.

Chris Hatch was a tall, lean guy with a head of thick, black hair that was starting to go silver at his temples. The silver hadn't been there when he'd first taken over the Portland office.

Like every other time Dante had been there, Hatch's office appeared to have been recently ransacked. In the age of computers and cloud storage, piles of paperwork, manila files, document envelopes, and god only knew what were stashed everywhere. Dante had asked him about it once and Hatch's response had been something like *good luck to anyone besides me who tries to find something.*

"You're going into witness protection," Hatch repeated as if Dante hadn't heard him the first time. Those had been Hatch's first words when he'd met Dante at the door.

"Hell to the *fuck no*," Dante said again.

Hatch sat behind his desk in a creaky chair that had seen better days. Too restless to sit, Dante stood across from him, arms crossed over his chest as he glared at his handler.

"Castone, be reasonable. Campos has nothing to lose and everything to gain. Daniella is in their crosshairs. He *will* find out about her. Maybe he doesn't know yet, but he will. WITSEC is the best place for both of you. When all this dies down, you'll be able to live your real life, Maybe, *maybe*, have an actual relationship. Who knows, stranger things have happened."

Dante's lips quirked at that last bit. He'd never been the relationship type.

"Aldo Campos was the brains behind this, we're sure of it. We're not sure who the trigger men were. But I promise you, we will find out."

If it had been Aldo behind his sister's death, Campos apparently did not understand that murdering Simone Maddison did not mean the case against him would fall apart. If anything, it would drive investigators and the prosecutor who took over to seal it up even more tightly. He'd be in jail for several lifetimes, instead of just one. Dante shouldn't be surprised by narcissistic criminals not understanding this truth, but he always was.

"Do they know she was there?" *They* being the killers.

It was much easier for Dante to let his entire being fill with rage than it was to think about never seeing the smiling eyes of his sister again. About never having Sunday night barbecues where they ordered takeout from the local barbecue joint because neither of them had the time to cook.

Hatch eyed him with compassion. "You know as well as I do that cops can't keep their damn mouths shut. There is no doubt in my mind that if they don't know already, they'll find out sooner rather than later."

Fuck compassion. Fuck cops who chatted among themselves. And especially, fuck Aldo Campos.

This weekend was supposed to have featured takeout and possibly catching some soccer matches on TV. A year ago, he might have thought about heading to André Dear's apartment, but the man had pulled a disappearing act last February. Dear had quit the Marshals Service and moved to some damp, moldy, flyspeck of a town on the Olympic Peninsula.

Cooper Fucking Springs.

Dante knew his way around the internet. He was very good at finding people who didn't want to be found. Truth be told, Dear wasn't even hiding from Dante. He was just out of reach. Which sucked because Dante had enjoyed his company.

He'd been pissed off and disappointed when he'd found out Dear had left town and without so much as a goodbye. But seeing as he was still UC at the time, there hadn't been much Dante could do about it. Certainly not after the fact. Maybe it had been his fault; it wasn't as if Dante was an easy man to get a hold of. But why Cooper Springs?

Turning in his chair, Hatch leaned down to grab a folder off the top of a seemingly random pile.

"Where's Daniella?" Dante had expected to find her stashed in an interview room or waiting for him in Hatch's office.

Looking up from the file, Hatch frowned.

"She's in protection, where you'll be joining her as soon as possible."

Hadn't they been through this already?

"No."

"No?" Hatch raised a dark eyebrow.

"What about the word is confusing? Two letters, one syllable. *No.*"

Hatch's nostrils flared as he did his best—Dante assumed anyway—to keep his temper in check.

"What the hell are you going to do, Dante? Campos is merciless. Simone didn't have a chance. It wasn't pretty."

That was below the belt. Dante stepped close enough to the desk so he could slightly lean over it. "Murder is rarely pretty, asshole." He didn't need a visual for what he suspected his sister had gone through.

Leaning back, Hatch lifted a hand in apology. "Sorry, that was unwarranted."

"I'll keep Daniella safe until the trial," Dante growled. "I won't let her down."

Hatch tapped the paperwork he held. "The new trial date hasn't been set yet, as I am sure you're aware. And whoever he paid is in the wind at the moment. How are you going to keep her safe from an enemy you can't identify?"

Why the fuck was Hatch arguing with him? They'd worked together for years; he should know better.

"You said that Daniella saw them. Has she seen a sketch artist yet? Where is she?" He looked around as if his niece was going to appear out of nowhere.

"Morrison and Walters have her safe. We were waiting for you to come in."

"What? And then you were going to send us to fucking Wisconsin or someplace?"

Hatch gave a head waggle. "Maybe not *Wisconsin*, but somewhere safer than Portland."

"No. Fuck, no." Dante had seen enough families—or what remained of them—whisked away from everything they knew. WITSEC was hard. Impossible even, unless the people involved were diligent and did their best to completely erase their former lives. Wisconsin or Kentucky or wherever Hatch had in mind, he and Daniella would be fish out of water.

Dante pressed his lips together and once again crossed his arms over his chest as they eyed each other. The office was quiet, the only sounds coming from the outside: cars driving by, horns honking. With a sigh, Hatch picked up his phone and punched in a set of numbers. At least he knew Dante well enough not to argue further.

While listening to Hatch speak to whoever was on the other end, an idea started unfolding in Dante's head. It involved a dark and rainy region of the Washington Coast and a silver fox of a man who liked to read cozy mysteries and drink tea.

Surely Cooper Fucking Springs would offer them the anonymity he and Daniella needed, as well as a way to *not* be sent away from everything they were both familiar with.

And a certain sexy ex-U.S. Marshal was the town's newest chief of police. Not that Dante was going to assume anything—or even alert Dear to their presence. Initially, Dante needed to focus on making sure Daniella stayed alive. And he needed to help her mourn. Maybe, when the dust had settled and everything was sorted out, he'd give André a call.

Hatch set the handset back down. "Alright, Dani is on her way. I hope you know what you're doing."

Dante didn't have an answer for that. He didn't know what he was doing. He'd never had kids. Dani was the only kid he knew.

"We'll sort it out."

"Call me if you need anything or if you change your mind. Maybe when this is all over, we can grab dinner."

A snort escaped Dante. This was uncharted waters for him. He had no idea what the future held—dinner plans were the least of his worries.

THREE

André - Late September

What the actual fuck?

André did not say those words out loud, but he thought them. Then he thought them again, louder, at the apparition standing at the back of the room.

What. The. Actual. Fuck?

Narrowing his eyes, André squinted over the heads of the Cooper Springs locals who'd filled The Steam Donkey that afternoon. All of them wanted an update on remains found near a popular hiking trail outside of town that morning. News traveled fast here. Wildfire fast.

Seriously, did he need a new eyeglasses prescription? The man standing at the back of the room with thick arms crossed over his chest and hair dark as a crow's wing gleaming under the lights couldn't be Dante Castone.

Could it?

No. It couldn't. This guy was a doppelgänger. The dim lighting around the doorway was making a man out of shadows. That's all it was.

"Chief Dear?" someone called from the audience. "What else can you tell us?"

Turning slightly, André forced his attention back to the crowd —and very much away from the possibility that someone who looked a lot like Dante Castone was leaning against the back wall. By the time he glanced toward the exit again, whoever it had been was gone.

Shadows playing tricks on him.

He'd either imagined him or André's subconscious was working overtime wishing for something it couldn't have.

Fifteen minutes later, André was back at the CS police station, sitting behind his desk and staring at the fake walnut-brown 1970s paneling opposite. The paneling had no answers for him and soon enough he'd be covering it up with his own André Dear-style murder board.

A quick search for Dante Castone had brought up nothing. At least, not for a Dante Castone living in the United States; there were a few in Italy. Calling the DEA and asking around for one of their undercover operatives would get him nowhere. The DEA was fiercely protective of their operatives and rightly so.

Memories from the last night he and Dante had spent together bloomed in his mind.

After not seeing him for weeks, André had figured they'd used up their time together. He'd berated himself for being upset about the end of something that had never had a label on it.

That last rainy evening they hadn't talked before falling into André's bed and sliding restlessly against each other's skin, aching for the physical pleasure they gave each other. He would never deny that the physical with Dante was good. Very good.

The reality was that an undercover DEA agent and U.S. Marshal were not long-term relationship material. André was not the type of person to demand someone change their career and Dante was not the type to just give up what he was driven to do.

The fact they'd gotten together at all was pure chance.

Opening his eyes again, André returned to the present, breathing in through his nose and letting the air back out slowly. He couldn't think about Dante Castone. He had a town to calm down. Murder was not what he'd expected when he'd decided to take the job, but maybe he should have.

Whose brilliant idea had it been to move to a small town and take over the vacant chief of police position anyway?

His. André had no one to blame but himself.

The thing was, he loved his new job ninety percent of the time. Being the chief of police in Cooper Springs was more fulfilling than he'd ever imagined. Sure, he spent a fair amount of time responding to calls about lost chickens and other animals—even horses, just like Jensen had said at his going-away party. Which was plain annoying because he hated that Jensen had called it. And domestic calls were never fun—unless he counted the time Hardy Phinney and Eustis Kurr got into a heated argument over the fact that Hardy had taken the batteries out of his hearing aid so he didn't have to listen to his equally cantankerous neighbor complain about the state of his front yard.

Furious, Eustis had dragged his push mower across their shared property line and proceeded to shorten the weeds enough that Hardy could see through his front window. Spotting his arch-enemy trespassing in his yard, Hardy had called the station, demanding someone come out and arrest Eustis.

Deputy Lani Cooper had filled André in before they'd arrived at the address together.

"You know those memes? 'He never married. Instead, he lived next to his best friend, and they did everything together?' That kind of thing?"

André nodded. He didn't spend much time on social media, but he had seen a meme or two like the one she was describing, the ones that pointed out gays, lesbians, and trans people had been around forever and living in plain sight.

"Hardy and Eustis are the living embodiment of that."

André opened his mouth to point out that Hardy had called the police on his supposed best friend.

"I know what you're about to say," she said, forestalling his remark. "Just believe me. They finish each other's sentences. When they come into town, they always arrive together. But they're both in their mideighties, and neither one of them has figured out how to tell the other one they care. I'd bet a dollar Eustis was worried about Hardy because he wasn't answering his phone or something."

"So... he decided to mow Hardy's lawn?"

Lani waggled her head and snickered. "Probably the grass was bugging him, too."

When they'd arrived at the address, André had immediately seen what Lani was talking about. The two octogenarians glared at each other from identical weather-beaten porches. And as he'd pretended to take Hardy's statement, the two men had interrupted each other and finished the other's sentences.

André had bitten the inside of his lip to keep from smiling as he listened to them. Even though each of the lots was over an acre in size, the houses themselves were barely one hundred feet apart and obviously designed by the same uninspired architect. He'd shaken his head, noting that Eustice's yard was painfully tidy. Hardy's was not.

Today, André had a real crime to solve.

Sitting forward, he planted his elbows on his desk, banging the wheels of his desk chair against the linoleum with a crash. Today's problem was not two grumpy old men. And it certainly wasn't Dante Castone. It couldn't be. Why Dante was *possibly*— André didn't know for sure—hanging around Cooper Springs was irrelevant.

What mattered going forward were the remains discovered on Crook's Trail behind town, between Cooper Springs and the much smaller town of Zenith. André had hiked the trail last summer just to prove to himself he could. He'd made it, but it hadn't been easy. While it started with a deceptively gentle slope, the forested path quickly steepened, becoming a never-ending series of brutal switchbacks that had him dripping with sweat and his thighs shaking from exertion. The climb had been worth it, though. The stunning view of the region on that sunny, clear day had been an incredible reward. And he knew now, from experience, that the hike was a lot of effort for someone who wanted to hide a body or other criminal activity.

André ran a hand through his cropped hair as he stared at the questions he'd jotted down after talking to the rangers—Critter and Mags—as well as Forrest Cooper and Rufus Ferguson. They all knew the area better than he did. As part of their job, Critter and Mags were on the trails regularly. He briefly wondered if they were somehow involved but quickly dismissed the thought.

How long had the bones been there? That was a question for the medical examiner. But André suspected at least a year, very possibly longer. From the description, the bones were already calcified.

Why hadn't anyone discovered the site before now? Critter and Mags thought the recent heavy rains were responsible. André would know more tomorrow after they hiked up and retrieved them.

At this point, he had to assume the worst, that the spot alongside a set of steep switchbacks was where the remains of the victim of a crime had been deposited. It was André's job to name the victim and do his best to bring them justice.

On that warm summer day, the old-growth forest had made an impression on him. The verdant moss was strewn over rocks and fallen tree trunks like a thick blanket and had beckoned him to sit and rest a while. The forest had been surprisingly noisy too, with various birds calling to each other as they hunted for bugs and other foodstuffs. He'd read that the Deep—as the center, untrodden parts of the forest where humans never went was called—was very quiet.

That summer afternoon, André had spotted a raven. Not that

he was a bird watcher, but the winged creature had been far too large to be a crow. André had read they nested in larger conifers, and the forest was full of trees with trunks so massive even two or three men couldn't wrap their arms around them. Their caw sounded like something out of a horror movie, nothing like a crow's.

Damn, tomorrow's retrieval hike was going to be wet and miserable. Fall had arrived, bringing with it copious amounts of rain, a constant cloud cover, and ever-shortening days.

A knock on the office door brought him back to the present. A second later, Lani poked her head around the doorframe. "Ready, boss? Jayden's waiting in the lobby."

Jayden Harlow, discoverer of the remains, was getting a special ride home. Back when André had been a kid—and dinosaurs roamed the earth—getting a ride from the police had been kind of cool. Not for him, of course, since his dad had been The Man. André didn't know how Jayden felt about it, but André was suspicious about his family situation. Why had the ninth grader been roaming Crook's Trail in nasty rainy weather? And on a school day?

André planned to talk to Jayden's mom, Lizzy, when he dropped him off. Just a check-in to see if he felt something was off. Lani's older brother, Forrest, had informed André that Jayden's dad was deployed overseas and therefore not around much. He suspected that basically being a single mom was hard on Lizzie. It wasn't easy being the wife of a deployed soldier, but something in Forrest's tone had told André he wasn't a fan of her personally.

But then, Forrest wasn't a fan of many people.

Jayden wasn't in trouble—not yet. But nothing good came out of skipping school. If André could keep one kid from making poor decisions, he was doing his job right. It would be more than anyone had done for Gene.

André pushed the memory of his younger brother back into

the mental box it belonged in. Some wounds just never healed. The only way to move on was to try and do better than the day before.

"Coming."

The teen sat hunched into one of the plastic chairs crammed in the station's "lobby" next to Carol Page's desk, which was currently unoccupied. André was dreading her upcoming vacation. Carol seemed to know everything about Cooper Springs. He was only keeping ahead of things because of her knowledge of the town and Lani's common sense.

Jayden glanced up when André entered the room, his expression wary.

"Ready to go home?" André asked.

Jayden shrugged, the wariness replaced by nonchalance. "I guess. Abby's probably worried."

"Who's Abby?" he asked.

He should know the answer. Wasn't that part of being a small-town sheriff?

"My little sister."

"Well, let's not keep her waiting any longer."

Zenith wasn't far from Cooper Springs as the crow (or raven) flew, but the road meandered through the forest land instead of going straight across it. It probably had started out as a path used by deer and elk and now, hundreds of years later, had evolved into a two-lane road that wound around the forest between the towns.

On the drive, André tried to draw Jayden out with innocuous questions, but the kid remained silent.

Only when they were rounding the last curve into Zenith did Jayden speak.

"How long have you been a cop?" he asked.

"I was a U.S. Marshal before taking this job, so law enforcement but not a police officer."

Jayden was quiet for a moment. André halted at the only stop sign in the town before continuing to Jayden's street.

"A U.S. Marshal? What was that like?"

"Like any job. Sometimes it was boring and sometimes it was more excitement than I needed."

"Like chasing down fugitives?" Jayden's tone was reverential.

Fucking Hollywood.

"Not like the movies—not most of the time anyway. But it was satisfying to know we got bad guys off the streets and into custody. I enjoyed being with the Marshals Service because I got to do a bit of everything. We were sometimes even loaned out to other agencies to help them bring in sex offenders or suspected murderers."

Flicking the indicator, he turned right onto a narrow residential street.

"What was the scariest case you were on?"

André actually couldn't talk about the scariest case, seeing as how it hadn't gone to trial yet. They would ask him to take the witness stand sometime in the next year, and he already wasn't looking forward to it. A few minutes later, André stopped the cruiser in front of a depressed-looking home. Hardy Phinney's yard looked like a master gardener's creation compared to the Harlows' lawn.

"You think I can have a word with your mom?"

"If she's home," Jayden said dismissively.

That didn't sound promising.

"Come on, let's get you inside."

Jayden's mother wasn't home. His sister Abby was.

"Jayden!" Abby said before bursting into tears and punching him in the chest.

"Ow, that hurt!" he complained, rubbing at the spot she'd nailed.

"You promised you wouldn't go up there again, but you did anyway. You promised!"

"Is your mom here?" André asked.

Abby shook her head, eyes still on Jayden.

André didn't like the fact that Ms. Harlow wasn't around and neither Abby nor Jayden seemed to know her whereabouts. Where was she that she hadn't heard about Jayden finding remains? Cell service was notoriously bad in the area, but surely she worried about her kids? It was close to dinnertime. Did these kids fend for themselves?

Knock it off, he told himself. Maybe Lizzy worked long hours. Jayden and Abby were obviously self-sufficient. Quit being so damn suspicious. He was just on edge because he thought he'd seen Dante Castone.

Which he hadn't.

André's suspicions rose again. Even Abby had heard about today's events. *Where was Lizzy?*

Jayden had the grace to hang his head as he rubbed the spot Abby had smacked. "I'm sorry, Abby. I really won't do it again."

Just how much time had Jayden been spending in the forest?

Abby's gaze at last flicked to André standing behind her brother.

"Did you get arrested???" she shrieked, her gaze locked on André.

Hastily, André plastered his most calming smile on his face.

"Jayden isn't under arrest or even in trouble. Not *much* trouble anyway. I just gave him a ride home. Do you know when your mom will be home?" He peered over the kids' heads, seeing only a sagging couch with an abandoned game controller sitting on it. A basket of clothes sat on a coffee table and a few moving boxes were shoved against a wall. Were they moving or had the boxes never been unpacked?

So many alarm bells were ringing.

The kids exchanged a glance. They were hiding something, but this wasn't the time to drag it out of them.

"Mom's not home right now," Abby said again. "She's usually here around dinnertime though."

The kids were both over the age of ten; legally, they could be left on their own.

André himself had survived with almost no parental oversight. He and Gene had been the ultimate latchkey kids with full run of the house until their dad got home in the evenings. For christ's sake, his dad hadn't known where André or Gene were most days of the week from fourth grade onward. The lack of structure had been fine for André; Gene, not so much.

"Alright, maybe just let her know I stopped by to introduce myself. I'll meet her another time." He glanced at Jayden. "No more treks in the forest and quit skipping school."

"Yessir."

"If you want to learn more about law enforcement, how about you drop by the station after school one of these days?"

"That might be cool," Jayden said in a grudging tone. The sparkle in his eyes told a different story.

André jogged down the walk to his cruiser and slid onto the driver's seat. He stared back at the run-down house, his index fingers tapping soundlessly against the steering wheel. Every instinct in him screamed that something was going on with the Harlow family. He'd check in with Carol and find out what he didn't know about the Harlows that he should.

FOUR

Dante – 4

"Please, Zio."

Daniella slow-blinked at him. Dante's heart stuttered and skipped a beat, as it had at least once or twice a day since that terrible night in August. The condition wasn't fatal. It was purely emotional and caused entirely by his niece. Daniella's dark brown eyes were replicas of her mother's.

"It's just two girls, Romy and Violet," she continued. "We're not going anywhere."

He opened his mouth, the words *hell* and *no* balancing on the tip of his tongue.

The aforementioned eyes glistened and shimmered slightly.

For fuck's sake. It wasn't even seven in the morning. A man needed warning to stave off an emotional assault like this one. Or at least a cup of fucking coffee.

How did parents not walk around their home muttering *fuck* every second of the day?

Running his hand through his hair, Dante resisted the urge to also tug on it. And say fuck. Was this what it was like parenting a teenager? Constantly toeing the line between yes and no? And her use of the Italian endearment for uncle? He was dead in the water. He was putty in her hands and Daniella knew it. How had his sister done it?

No. He was not going there. Not this morning. The grief and guilt over Simone's death—murder—had a way of dragging him under until he felt like he couldn't breathe.

Dante drew a strengthening breath in through his nose. He had to rally against this onslaught. He started to speak, but his niece beat him to it.

"All I ever do is go to school and come back here. It's not even a home!"

Were those tears glimmering in her eyes? Dante refused to glance around the shabby rental house. The owner had advertised it as furnished. Along with the very basic bedroom sets and kitchenware, the house had come with a garishly bright, pink floral couch and settee, the ugliest living room furniture Dante had ever laid eyes on—and that was saying a lot.

It was, however, the best he'd been able to do at short notice, what with hiding from hardened criminals and wanting to keep Daniella alive without going into witness protection. They could still go, the offer was open, but neither of them wanted to run away to Wisconsin or Vermont.

There was truth in Daniella's words, though. The two-bedroom rambler was nothing like the beautiful Tudor home Daniella had lived in with her mother or the condo Dante owned in Portland that was now gathering dust. He hadn't even returned home to pack his belongings. Life was on hold until the depraved scumbags who'd murdered Simone were dead or behind bars for the rest of their lives.

"Daniella," he began sternly, wishing the coffee maker would hurry the fuck up, "we have to be watchful. Even here in tiny

Cooper Springs, someone we don't want to might recognize you or me."

Someone *had* recognized Dante, but he refused to let the infuriatingly sexy police chief hijack this conversation. All thoughts of André Dear, please exit stage left. It was too fucking early.

It was possible that Simone's murderer didn't know what Dante looked like, or even that Simone had a brother. She had been a busy prosecutor, and Dante had been working undercover. But now the killers did know that Simone had a kid.

As little as he and Dani had talked about it, Dante knew the timeline of the evening.

Not wanting to interrupt if it was one of Simone's work colleagues, Daniella had paused on the landing. From her vantage point, she'd been able to see the two men on the other side of the threshold and had watched in horror as one of them raised a shotgun, aimed it at her mother's chest, and pulled the trigger.

Daniella had told Dante it felt like all the oxygen was sucked out of her lungs, like she was suffocating and exploding at the same time, and that she probably couldn't have screamed even if she had wanted to. But she must have made some sort of noise.

The man holding the gun had taken a step into the entry, his attention on Daniella frozen in the shadows. He'd probably intended to take care of loose ends, but a late-night jogger had run by on the sidewalk in front of the house. The good Samaritan must have sensed something was wrong because he stopped, came back to the end of their walkway, and then called out.

The shooter had pointed two fingers first at himself and then toward Daniella. Both men then escaped across the lawn and into the night. They were still at large. The killers' heads had been covered with knit caps and they'd worn anonymous black clothing, but Daniella reported she had seen parts of the shooter's face. She'd spent hours with a sketch artist, but what she remembered hadn't led to an ID or even a suspect.

"We could be recognized anywhere!" Daniella cried, bringing Dante back to the present. "I go to school. What about someone seeing me there? I just want to hang out with friends. I can't live in... in a jar all the time. And Romy's nice."

A jar? Dante side-eyed the coffee maker, wondering if there was a Fast setting he'd missed. He needed all the caffeine in his bloodstream now.

"She invited me to sit at her table during lunch, and all we're going to do is watch TV and stuff."

Why the hell was locking Daniella up in her room frowned upon, anyway? How did parents deal with releasing their children into the wild where anything could happen to them?

"Please?"

Those damn eyes. Dante was going to cave. He was going to say yes, she could go to her new friend's house after school. His niece was right. It was impossible to protect her at all times. He had an obligation to his dead sister to keep her child safe, but also happy too. Daniella was the only family he had left, and he damn well wasn't letting anything happen to her. Literally over his dead body.

Those pleading brown eyes.

"Okay."

"Yes!" Daniella spun in a circle, ending her dance with a fist pump toward the ceiling.

"But"—he jabbed his index finger toward her—"you do not go anywhere else. You don't pass Go. You don't collect two hundred dollars. No car ride with someone except me. No impulse trip to the mall. No changing your mind and going to a different house. I need all Romy's contact information and I need to talk to her parents. And you have to remember not to talk about your mom or Portland. Those are the rules."

"Zio... there's no mall in this town."

"No stopping at the pizza place after school."

That's where a lot of high schoolers hung out after classes. Dante figured it was because the food was cheap, not because it was good. Cooper Springs needed decent pizza.

His niece eyed him. He stared back. Seeming to realize her uncle wasn't budging on this, she sighed. "Fine. I agree. Romy's dad is the shop teacher at school, Mr. Barone. He's not some serial killer."

Ah, yes. Dante recalled meeting Barone at The Steam Donkey when news had broken that a kid had found bones up on the mountains. His first impression was that Barone was an alright guy. The man hadn't screamed criminal to him—or serial killer, for that matter. But then, serial killers often hid in plain sight.

"Have your friend text you her dad's phone number and address *before* you go over there, then forward it to me. And I'll be picking you up promptly at nine." That was the other drawback of this town. The cell service was terrible.

Internally, Dante rolled his eyes at himself. How the tables had turned. At her age, Dante had been out late, sometimes all night, and never bothered checking in with his family. At her age, he'd thought he was invincible and smarter than everybody else. Simone had been out of the house already. Truthfully, Dante crashing with his friends had been a survival tactic.

"Okay." She nodded. "Thank you, Zio." Daniella dipped her chin and did a weird shrug thing that Dante couldn't interpret.

"Thank you for what?" he asked, eyeing her warily.

The caffeine machine continued to burble and spit but the magic *it's done* light hadn't turned green yet. He was sorely tempted to grab the carafe and pour some into his waiting mug. But the last time he'd done that, the machine hurled hot water and coffee grounds all over the kitchen counter and floor.

"Thank you for not making me go into foster care or witness protection. Thanks for being the best zio ever."

"Baby girl." His chest hurt. Dante knew how the Grinch felt when his heart expanded—it fucking *hurt*. Dante wasn't one for big emotional scenes, but Daniella was doing her best to get him there. He reached out, intending to take her into a hug.

She drew back, a horrified expression on her face, her eyebrows scrunching together.

"I am *not* a baby girl. It's sexist. And creepy, too." The added growl reminded Dante very much of Simone. "You should know better."

Oh, for the *fucking* love of god, was *he* going to survive raising Daniella to adulthood? He needed one of those magic eight ball things to help him out. If there were such a thing as ghosts, then Simone's was in the kitchen laughing her ass off at him right now.

Friday had finally arrived, and, against Dante's better judgment, Daniella was spending the night with Romy. Earlier in the week while Dani was at school, Dante had driven by the tiny house Romy lived in just to check it out.

The house itself was fine. Their neighbor appeared to be some sort of sculpture artist as that lawn was full of wooden eagles in midflight, bears in all sorts of poses, some sort of merman, and even what Dante suspected was supposed to be a Sasquatch. Cooper Springs was definitely unique. At least he knew there were makeshift weapons at hand if the girls needed them.

He'd run a cursory background check on Vincent Barone too. Maybe not standard guardian behavior, but a paranoid uncle was all Daniella had standing between her and some Very Bad People. And he'd be damned if something happened to her because he'd been careless about her safety.

Not that he expected them to come after her here in Cooper Springs, almost two hundred miles from Salem, but it never hurt to be prepared. Hypervigilant? Absolutely.

Dante shifted in the driver's seat as he stared out the windshield at a different house. He was also horny. And the horny part had definitely hijacked Dante's common sense tonight. He had an evening to himself for the first time in three months and knew exactly what he wanted to do with it.

Or who.

Not only had Dante researched the shop teacher, but he'd given into the need to root out Dear's new home address. Last night he'd assured himself he was just curious as his fingers flew across the keys and he pressed Enter, waiting for the numbers he wanted to pop up on his screen. He wasn't going to do anything with the information, of course; he just wanted to have it.

Just curious.

That had been the first lie he'd told himself. The second lie had been that he was just going to drive by and see for himself what kind of place André lived in now. That's what he was telling himself tonight. The first, second—and third—times he'd passed the practical wood-shingled home André lived in, it had been dark, and no car had been parked on the street out front. Now there was a light on inside. It called to Dante like some sort of beacon.

"I am so fucked," he muttered to himself.

Seeing André Dear kitted out in a police chief's togs and standing in front of the crowd at The Steam Donkey had about undone Dante. He'd forced himself to stand at the back of the room, but André had seen him too. Disbelief had flashed across his face before his expression shuttered and he started taking questions about the remains found in the woods.

Dante had a weakness for a man in uniform. Add a crisp shirt and slacks to his already established weakness for André Dear, and he was done for. Of course, his current situation was his own fault since he was the one who'd declined witness protection and moved Daniella to tiny Cooper Springs instead of Minnesota. It had been easy enough for Dante to ferret out André's new job.

And once he had the information, there was no way he was heading anywhere else.

"What do I think I'm doing?" He asked himself as he stopped at the curb in front of a parked minivan. "If Dear wanted me to know where he was going back in February, he would have told me."

But he hadn't.

The wind buffeted the car and dots of moisture smacked against his windshield, beaded, and began rolling downward. Dante continued to stare at the tidy bungalow.

Admittedly, being undercover meant only serious emergencies —like his sister being murdered—were communicated to him. And they'd never had that kind of relationship anyway. Dante had showed up when he had an itch to scratch and that was the extent of it.

But was that really true?

Last year, knocking on André's door and having it answered by a thirty-something woman with a kid peeking out from behind her had been a shock. An unpleasant one. The man had moved away with no notice, and Dante had at first been worried and then hurt. His own reaction had been a surprise to him, forcing him to admit to himself that—*against his better judgment*—he harbored complicated, unexpected, and unacknowledged feelings for André Dear.

Sure, their relationship had had prescribed limits because of Dante's undercover work, but these *emotions* had snuck up on him anyway. And *maybe* his last visit to Dear's apartment had been fueled by the idea that there could be something more between them, something maybe worth giving up undercover ops for. That *maybe* his vague plan, one that involved Dante coming out into the open, possibly switching to the Marshals Service like André, had been less about walking away from the grime of UC work and more about walking to whatever the two of them could maybe have together.

That was a lot of maybes.

But he'd needed to finish that assignment. And when he'd surfaced again and shown up on that doorstep, André had been long gone. So he'd taken another UC assignment in eastern Oregon.

"I'll just knock on the door," Dante said out loud, shutting off the engine. "If he wants me to leave, I'll leave."

Second-guessing his decision, but not enough to stop himself, Dante opened the car door and climbed out. The shades were drawn, so Dante couldn't see inside, but behind them, a shadowy figure crossed the room and lowered itself down.

The wind gusted again, plastering his jacket against his back as he stared at the house. Down the street, a gate rattled. Dante shivered and hunched his shoulders against the chill.

It was easy to imagine André tucked into his couch, his reading glasses perched on his nose, a book in one hand and a cup of tea sitting on the end table. There was only one way to find out if he was right. Dante climbed the three steps to the porch, lifted his fist, and knocked.

When the door opened just moments later, Dante found himself as close to André Dear as he had been in months. He must have recently taken a shower; his hair was still slightly damp. Instinctively, Dante breathed in, filling his lungs with the scent of him, a combination of spicy aftershave and the last traces of lavender body soap that was uniquely André.

"Dante," André said, almost as if he'd been expecting him.

"André." Dante was at a loss for words. He should have planned this better.

"What do you want?"

André's glasses were perched on the top of his head. His uniform had been replaced with jeans and a white t-shirt. His feet were bare, even though it was October. Dante's cock twitched.

He'd promised himself he wouldn't go all caveman when he

got the chance to talk to André again. Resolve crumbled into dust. Dante wanted André Dear naked. He wanted to make the man beg and make him promise that he'd be there the next time Dante came over. That never again would Dante knock on a door and have it answered by the wrong person.

FIVE

André

Again, he'd known it was Dante before he opened the door. The man couldn't just knock. The sound had to be an authoritative announcement of his presence, a demand to enter. André briefly considered pretending he wasn't home, but a heady mix of anticipation, desire, and curiosity won over self-preservation.

"André." Dante growled his name, pushing past him into the house as if he belonged there.

André shut and relocked the door before turning to face his "guest."

Damn the man. The minute André had spotted him at The Steam Donkey last month, he'd wanted to wrap his arms around him, breathe his scent in, and never let him go. He had tried to convince himself it wasn't Castone, but he'd known the truth. His reaction had been ridiculous because they'd meant nothing beyond a good lay to each other.

"I don't know if this is a good idea." André was at least going to try and do the right thing.

"Of course, it's not a fucking good idea," Dante agreed pleasantly, closing the distance between them again. Dante's scent, a blend of the aftershave he used—something with spice—and sweat, had André's dick very happy. "That's never stopped us before."

It hadn't. He opened his mouth, intending to add more to his protest, but he was too slow, addled by Dante's presence in his house. A hand grabbed his chin, holding him still. Rough lips pressed against his, then Dante's tongue flicked across his mouth, leaving fire in its wake as he demanded another form of entrance.

"God, André," Dante groaned. "I need this so much."

André couldn't argue; hell, he couldn't speak. There was no point in trying to hide the fact that he wanted Dante too. Wrapping his arms around Dante's waist and grabbing his tight ass, André pulled the other man's body flush against his. They were both fully clothed, but the press of Dante's cock against his own erection was fucking heaven. And history told him they would be naked soon enough.

Getting their clothes off and being skin against skin was the priority. Whatever reason Dante had for showing up they could talk about later. *Afterward.*

"Clothes off," André hissed.

"Yes," Dante agreed.

Thick fingers and clumsy thumbs tugged at buttons, snaps, and belt loops. Impatience winning out, André pushed Dante's hands away to shove his own jeans and briefs down, finally kicking them off and away. Even more quickly, he pulled his t-shirt over his head. The offending shirt caught on his reading glasses and flung them to the floor, where they landed with a clatter.

A second later, Dante's shirt, jeans, and boxer briefs landed on the same pile.

"Jesus, André, you look good." Dante's electric-blue eyes were dark with need. "Good enough to eat."

André's cock twitched at his words and at the sight of him

naked. In André's humble opinion, Dante Castone was a work of art. The dusting of dark chest hair became thicker as it headed downward to cover his cock and beefy thighs. When they'd first hooked up, André had felt lesser, too old. His own lean runner's physique, graying head of hair, and sparse body hair made him self-conscious, but Dante had kept coming back—until he hadn't —so there must have been something the younger man liked about him.

"Where's your bedroom?" Dante rasped. "We don't want to give the neighbors a show."

André gestured behind him toward a hallway that led away from the kitchen.

"Second door on the left."

Following his direction, Dante started toward the bedroom with André on his heels.

"Nice," Dante said once they were inside. André wasn't sure what was nice about it. It was a boring room with a boring queen-size mattress covered with a bland comforter and two pillows.

"I haven't had time to do much."

"S'okay, you should see my place."

It shocked André to realize he wanted to see Dante's home. He wanted to know where the man lived. Did he have a book-shelf? Did the man even read? André had no idea. They'd never let themselves get to know each other that way. He knew Dante's body, but he wanted to learn the rest of him.

Which was why he'd left before and why this was such a bad idea now.

Just this once.

Flinging the comforter aside, André lay down on the bed, propping himself up on one elbow and watching Dante.

"You've got supplies?" Dante asked.

André nodded at his bedside table. They'd never gotten past using condoms. When he'd moved, André had left them in the drawer. And he hadn't had sex since the last time Dante left without warning. Had Dante? André realized he didn't want to know.

Cocking one knee, he reached down to stroke himself, watching through half-shut eyes while Dante got out the condoms and lube. He shot André an unreadable look as he set one foil packet within reach.

"What?" André asked.

"Mm, nothing." The mattress dipped when Dante lay down next to him. He batted André's hand away from his erection. "Leave that to the experts. That's me, I'm the expert."

"Prove it."

A smile stretched Dante's lips.

"At your service."

The next thing stretching Dante's lips was André's cock.

"Holy fuck," André nearly shouted.

The heat of his mouth, the way he flicked and licked André's tip with his tongue before sucking and releasing—André had missed this. He'd missed the way Dante revved his engine. From zero to fucking sixty.

Clawing at the sheets, André did his best not to come right away. He wanted to savor this moment. Who knew when it would happen again? Dante was taking him as far down his throat as he could, his nose deep in André's groin. André was lost to the sensation, his hips thrusting as the spark of orgasm grew stronger.

"Dante," he managed. "Fuck me now."

Letting André's cock slip out of his mouth, Dante raised himself onto his elbows.

"Normally I'd take that as a challenge, but it's been a long damn time." With the skill of an expert, Dante rolled on the condom before squeezing lube onto his fingers. "Roll over so I can get to that sexy ass."

André rolled onto his front and pulled his knees underneath him. His throbbing cock brushed against the sheet, pure torture.

"Damn, you're even hotter than I remembered."

Cool, slick-covered fingers began circling and massaging André's entrance. He wanted more right away, but it had been too long since he'd done this. Snaking a hand underneath his body, he wrapped his fingers around his cock and pumped himself while Dante teased him. Not enough to come, but enough to keep him close.

"Ready?"

André nodded, his cheek smashed against the sheet as he kept his hand moving. Dante's thick finger eased inside his body, slowed, and then moved past the most resistant muscle. André shifted to accommodate him. He couldn't stop himself from pressing back, pushing himself further—he needed *more*.

Dante pulled his hand back. André panicked, but his lover was just adding a second digit, stretching him further.

"I need you so bad," Dante whispered against his ear. "Can't wait to feel that heat around my cock. Want to pound that ass, watch my fat cock hammering in and out of that hole."

"God, yes, please fucking fuck me now."

He pushed his hips backward again and used his free hand to pull one ass cheek aside. Anything to get more.

This time it was Dante who moaned just as his questing fingers rasped across André's prostate. André shouted. No sentences, just begging and want, and *more* and *please don't stop*. Somehow, though, he had the wherewithal to fist his cock in a tight grip and keep himself from coming.

The fingers pulled out of his ass, leaving him briefly empty and needy. He didn't have to wait more than a few seconds before Dante's cock was tapping against his entrance and pushing inside him. Dante seemed to remember that André liked it slow. He reveled in the vague burn and resistance his ass offered while Dante burrowed further into his body. *Resistance is futile.*

Strong fingers gripped his hips, holding him in place. André arched his back and spread his knees, taking Dante as far inside as he could.

"Oh god, oh god, oh god," he babbled, all semblance of control and actual speech gone.

"I'm trying to go slow, but," Dante groaned, his hips jerking against André's, "I don't know how long I can hold out. I fucking love this."

"Just... fuck me." Dante shoved inside him again, going deep, scraping across the bundle of nerves that set André on fire. "I'm gonna come. I can't, oh fuck..."

Dante kept pounding into him. To André, it seemed like he could feel everything everywhere all at once. Dante's cock stretching his hole. The bristly scrape of pubes against his ass. Beads of sweat dripping from Dante's forehead—even though it was late October and not warm at all. The air in the bedroom had heated, caressing both their bodies.

They were setting their own inferno.

Dante groaned again, deep and growly, so deep André felt the sound in his chest, and then the condom was filling with the warmth of Dante's come. André's balls were rock hard, and the spark at the base of his spine was ready to burst into flame. Jamming a hand underneath himself again, André intended to stroke himself to completion. But Dante managed a series of frenzied thrusts that launched André over the edge before he could.

Come gushed over his fingers and onto the sheets, and André had the random thought he was going to need to change them later.

After Dante left again.

Shit.

Mercifully, there was no emergency call from dispatch in the night. After the last few weeks filled with fielding panicked calls from Cooper Springs residents about the remains, André needed a break. Lani didn't expect him in until the afternoon. Fingers crossed, there would continue to be no emergencies and he could spend the morning brooding about Dante.

Dante, who'd stayed the night.

It was only five a.m. André supposed staying the night was a stretch of the imagination. He glanced out the kitchen window where there was nothing but darkness; the sun wasn't even hinting that it might be up soon. And Dante Castone was still in André's bed.

That hadn't happened often. Usually he was gone before André woke.

Just in case he'd imagined him, André padded back to his bedroom door and peeked inside. Dante was sprawled face down, a pillow over his head, and the blankets pulled up so only the tip of his chin was visible.

Yep. He was really still there.

Back in the kitchen, André poured himself a cup of coffee and stood at the counter eating a quick breakfast of granola with yogurt mixed in. He was going to have to take a dreaded trip to the grocery store. The whole Dante thing was throwing him off his stride. Normally he'd have already gone for a run, done something to burn off the excess energy that was thrumming across his skin.

Maybe it was his body still reacting to all the attention last night. He wasn't complaining. Dante in his bed had been the cause of two orgasms and the best night's sleep he'd had in months.

A muffled thump followed by soft footsteps told him Dante was awake. The bathroom door shut and soon enough he heard the sound of the toilet flushing and the sink running. André's stomach twisted as he readied himself for the inevitable "see you later" conversation.

Dante stepped into the kitchen. Aside from the jeans he'd

been wearing the night before, he'd found one of André's older Marshals Service sweatshirts.

"I hope you don't mind," Dante said, his voice a bit hoarse.

"No," André replied while trying not to swallow his tongue at the sight of Dante's chest challenging the confines of his shirt. What was it about a man—specifically that man—wearing his clothes? It was just a ratty sweatshirt, not a wedding ring. "Coffee?" he offered, turning away from the distraction that was Dante to grab a second mug from the cupboard.

"God, yes."

"Milk or anything?" For fuck's sake, he didn't even know if the man took cream in his coffee. The realization was a welcome dash of cold water over his soft romantic thoughts. He needed to be focusing on the remains, the Harlow family, the prowlers north of town, the HR issue that was Deputy Trent—not fucking Dante Castone. Both literally and figuratively.

"Just plain, thanks."

André busied himself pouring a black cup of coffee and shoving his wishful thinking back into the box where it belonged. He reminded himself why he'd taken the police chief's position in Cooper Springs—to start new, not to fall back into an old, unhealthy habit. As he handed the steaming mug to Dante, their fingers brushed against each other, sending a shock of electricity directly to André's heart.

"So, why are you in Cooper Springs?" *And when are you leaving...* André left that part implied.

Instead of answering, Dante sipped at his coffee. "Good coffee."

"Of course, it's good coffee. What do you think I am, a monster?"

"I dunno. Cops, we get used to shit coffee and think it's normal."

It was true. LEOs got used to a lot of stuff that the regular population would never put up with. Bad coffee, crap meals, no sleep, interrupted sleep, lying liars who lied.

"Why are you here, in my house, in Cooper Springs?"

Carefully, Dante set his mug down on the counter. André sensed there was an internal debate happening—how much was Dante willing to reveal?

Instead of looking at André, Dante stared out the kitchen window. André noted that it was starting to get light.

"I'm not with the DEA any longer. No more undercover work for me."

"Why? What happened?" Had he been found out by whoever he'd been investigating?

"My sister was killed," His tone was flat. *Just the facts, ma'am.* Stunned as he was by the information, André realized the words were acting as a dam, holding back emotions André doubted Dante would ever willingly reveal. "I'm my niece's only relative— the only relative my sister would trust her daughter with anyway —so now I'm her guardian. Can you imagine?" he said with a soft snort. "Me? The guardian of a fifteen-year-old girl?"

"She's here in Cooper Springs with you?"

"Of course, she's here. Did you think I left her behind? She goes to the high school."

"No, I didn't think you left her behind. I'm just a bit shocked. I didn't know you had a sister. I'm sorry for your loss—and for your niece."

"Yeah, I'm fucking sorry too. Imagine having me for an uncle. Imagine having your world disintegrate around you and I'm the only one you have to hold things together."

André moved without thinking, stepping into Dante's space. "Honestly, I know nothing about you. Not really. But I bet you're exactly what your niece needs."

They stared at each other without touching, as much as André wanted to.

"Why did you come here last night?" he asked.

Dante's lips quirked. "I thought I made that obvious."

Booty call.

"You can't keep coming over," André said firmly. Dante may light him up faster than a barbecue doused in kerosene, but sex did not a relationship make.

"Daniella is at a friend's house," Dante said, instead of agreeing with André. Now Dante crowded in against him, maneuvering André backward until his ass was pressed against the counter behind him. "I couldn't think of anything else I wanted to do. Ever since the day I saw you in The Steam Donkey, wearing your police chief's outfit, looking calm, cool, and collected, I've been dreaming about peeling your clothes off and having my way with you."

André was hard already. All he needed was for Dante to be in his proximity and his cock sprang to attention. With a needy groan, he pressed his lips against Dante's—if nothing else, to get the man to stop talking. Dante grunted as he leaned into André's kiss, sliding his hands underneath the long-sleeved t-shirt he wore.

By the time they got back to the bedroom, they were naked again and André was ready to beg. Dante spun him around and lay down on the bed.

"Fuck me, André. Fuck me hard."

The words sent such a surge of lust through his system that André wrapped his fingers around his cock to ensure he didn't come on the spot. He and Dante had always traded, there'd been no top-bottom roles, but Dante asking for it so directly? That was new.

André climbed onto the bed and crawled over to where Dante lay. He hovered over his body for a moment, taking in his masculine beauty.

"Sometime this century would be nice," Dante said.

"Asshole."

Then André proceeded to fuck Dante into the mattress.

SIX

Dante

By the time Dante recovered from his third orgasm in just about twelve hours, it was after nine on Saturday morning.

"Shit," he muttered after seeing the time. "I have to pick up Daniella."

"Mm," André murmured.

Dante glanced at his—at André. He had one arm thrown over his face so Dante couldn't read his expression. Dante wasn't sure why, but the arm over the face bothered him. Unfortunately, he didn't have the time this morning to try and solve the puzzle box that was André Dear. He doubted he could do it in a day anyway. Heaving himself out of bed for the second time that day, he relocated the clothes he'd been wearing last night and put them back on.

"Do you think Daniella will notice these are the same clothes I was wearing when I dropped her off?" he asked, looking down at his rumpled shirt and jeans.

André moved his arm away from his eyes to take in Dante's apparel. "She's fifteen?"

Dante nodded.

"Yep."

"Damn. I'll just tell her I overslept."

Dante rarely overslept but Daniella didn't know that.

"I'm sure that'll work."

André's mood *had* changed, but Dante didn't have the time to analyze why. He couldn't be late picking up Daniella. He'd gotten stuck in traffic once when they'd first moved to Cooper Springs and had been five minutes behind schedule. By the time he arrived at the high school, Daniella had almost been in tears. The grief counselor she was seeing in Aberdeen seemed to be good at her job, but the situation was not helped by the fact that Dani couldn't be open about her mourning. Not even the counselor knew her mother had been murdered, not killed in a car accident.

"I'll see you later," he said, patting himself to make sure he had his wallet and cell phone. Check to both. The sense of calm he'd woken up with? That had evaporated.

André slipped off the bed, reaching down to drag on the gray sweatpants he'd been wearing earlier. Dante had a weakness for men in sweatpants—hell, he had a weakness for André. The sweatshirt Dante had borrowed for a few minutes lay on the floor. Picking it up, André tossed it in a dirty clothes hamper near the closet. Dante felt a stab of disappointment; he'd hoped André would wear it.

Yes, he was possessive.

"There's an Elma-Cooper Springs makeup game tonight," André said. "The department will be busy. Who knew small-town football would be such an issue?"

"Oh, come on, even I know small towns live and breathe their home teams. Daniella's been talking about it," he said as he left André's bedroom and headed down the hall toward the front door. "I'm pretty sure even she wants to go."

"It's bound to be a good one," André said matter-of-factly. "Well," he added after a second, "entertaining anyway."

Dante opened the door, his gut telling him they should be talking about something other than high school football, but for the life of him, he didn't know how to bridge the gap. Somehow they'd gone from great sex to casual-friend conversation, and he didn't know how to get to where he really wanted to be. Which was in André's bed. Permanently.

He stepped out onto the small porch and the door shut softly behind him. André did not say goodbye.

"Dammit."

But he didn't have time to worry about André. He needed to pick up Daniella.

～

Several weeks passed relatively drama free—drama, Dante was quickly learning, was an integral part of teenager life. And, even though he wanted to, Dante had not stopped by André's again. The want was there and almost painful. Like those commercials where kids stared in a window at all the toys they wanted but couldn't have. He'd realized he needed to be subtle in his approach to André. He needed to court the sexy police chief instead of showing up uninvited and making him feel like all Dante wanted was sex.

He definitely wanted sex too, but he also wanted the rest of André Dear.

More recently, the shit in Cooper Springs had hit the fan and Dante figured André wouldn't be amenable to him stopping by. The body of a local, Lizzy Harlow, had been discovered on the town's beach by a realtor and, of all people, Romy Barone's dad. Technically, she had been found by Xavier Stone's dog, but that was semantics.

The Thanksgiving holiday had come and gone as well—and good fucking riddance too. He and Daniella had spent it together, just the two of them in the crappy rental house with the heinous floral couch. Daniella had laughed at Dante's attempt to make homemade gnocchi for their dinner. Not for the first time, he'd wished his grandmother was still alive so he could watch her competent hands form the potato flour-based pasta. His gnocchi looked like a science experiment gone very wrong.

He'd make bad gnocchi for the rest of his life if it made his niece laugh. And at least it had been edible.

Dante sighed, trying not to think about the fucking Christmas holiday that loomed ahead. Winter vacation had started that day, which meant two weeks of Daniella at home, missing her mom and her friends from her old life.

While Daniella was in school, Dante spent most of his time tracking down any information he could about The Fucking Murderer, Aldo Campos, and his equally heinous brother, Alonso. But, with his niece at home for the rest of the year, he would be forced to abandon the search until after New Year's. Not that he was having much success anyway.

He'd circled around the idea that he should come clean to André about the self-imposed witness protection he and Dani were in, but the man was knee-deep in a murder investigation of his own and didn't need the distraction of Dante's problems. At least, that's what Dante told himself.

And anyway, asking for André's help would just be an excuse to see him. The likelihood that he didn't want Dante stopping by for what André thought was casual sex was probably closer to the truth. Dante still hadn't figured out how to bring up wanting more than that, especially since the chief of police seemed to disappear around the nearest corner anytime Dante was around.

"Zio," Daniella said from the passenger seat. "Have you thought any more about us getting a dog?"

Seriously? While he was driving?

Dante could feel his niece's eyes on him. He stared at the road in front of them. The road that led directly past the sign for the Humane Society.

"Today? Right now?" They'd talked about it. Or, rather, Dani had brought the subject up one morning a few weeks ago, before Dante'd had any coffee.

"Please?" she wheedled. "I'd feel safer with a dog. You wouldn't have to stay home all the time if we had a dog. And I'd be able to walk it and not worry. Don't you always say that burglar alarms are nothing compared to an old-fashioned dog?"

Dante wracked his brains but couldn't come up with an argument.

To her credit, Daniella waited for his answer without wavering. Dante steeled himself, working up the courage to say no. He didn't want a pet. It was hard enough taking care of Daniella. Parenting was incredibly stressful.

Maybe he needed to take up yoga or something to relax him. Sex would be good, but there was only one person he wanted that with. From Dear's expression the last time he'd managed to catch his eye, before André found a corner to disappear around, Dante figured the man would rather punch him than go to bed with him.

No thinking about sex around his niece.

She was right. He had said dogs were better than alarm systems. And it was true. But having his niece repeat the words back to him in order to get her own way was beyond brutal. Especially when she was probably resorting to puppy-dog eyes. He kept his own firmly on the highway.

"Research says that walking a dog is one of the best things for mental health."

It was as if she could sense him weakening.

He was a sucker.

"I'll think about it," he replied, shooting a quick glance at his niece.

A small smile played across Daniella's lips. "Zio, everyone knows 'I'll think about it' means 'yes.'"

Damn. He'd hoped Daniella would forget about wanting a pet.

Why couldn't she want something simple? Like a goldfish? Or a pet rock? He'd had one of those in elementary school and it hadn't died. Although his fuckass of a brother had thrown it into the ravine behind their house, so in a way it had died.

It was difficult enough learning how to grocery shop for the two of them, which is where they were headed now, not the Humane Society. The grocery store. Hell on earth in Dante's opinion, but a necessary one.

"Romy—" Daniella began.

"Please, Daniella, don't start with how Romy has a dog. We are not like them."

There was a palpably hurt silence. Shit. Dante gripped the steering wheel and opened his mouth to apologize.

"Romy doesn't have a dog," his niece said before he could say a word, "but Mr. Barone's boyfriend and his mom both do, and Romy gets to walk them all the time."

One of those dogs had found Lizzy Harlow.

"Right." Now he felt like complete shit. The worst uncle on the planet. Definitely didn't deserve to be called zio.

"But I would feel even safer with a dog. And you wouldn't have to stay home all the time. I mean, what if you want to go on a date or something?"

Dante wanted to shut his eyes, but he was driving and had no desire to end up in a ditch. Daniella knew Dante was gay, he'd never hidden it from her, or anyone for that matter. But he wasn't talking about his love life with a nearly sixteen-year-old girl.

They passed the Gray's Harbor Humane Society sign. The rest of the drive to the grocery store was completed in silence. The only sounds came from the car's tires on the road and the swish of the windshield wipers trying to keep the raindrops at bay.

Out of habit, he parked at the back of the lot, away from other vehicles.

"Why do we always have to park way out here?" Daniella

complained as they trudged through the rain to the store's entrance.

"So I can better see who's coming after us," Dante replied honestly.

He immediately felt guilty, even if it was the truth.

Daniella slowed her steps. "Do you think the men who killed Mom will find us here?"

"They might. But they may think we ran to the East Coast. We just need to be diligent until they're caught."

"Do you think they will be caught?"

"Criminals like them are stupid, foolish men. Eventually, they won't be able to stand it any longer and will brag to the wrong person that they were responsible for Simone's death. Law enforcement will pick them up and that will be that." Dante hoped so anyway. "Until that happens though, I am going to be as safe as possible. If that means parking a mile from the entrance to the grocery store so no one can ambush us, then that's what I will do."

Daniella didn't respond but she did pick up the pace again. Soon enough, they were inside under the fluorescent lights of the grocery store, picking out things normal families ate, like apples and bananas, and checking the price of frozen turkey. Dante hated turkey, but he'd buy it for his niece.

"One of us is going to have to learn how to really cook," Dante teased as they headed down the baking aisle so he could grab a bag of 00 flour off the shelf. At least the store sold proper flour for pizza dough. That he did know how to make.

"We could watch YouTube videos."

"Yeah, not gonna happen."

Paying attention to Daniella instead of where he was heading, Dante pushed the cart around the corner and straight into the Cooper Springs police chief.

"Oh, shit, sorry," Dante said, backing the cart up. Dark circles stood out underneath André's eyes. The man wasn't getting enough rest. "You look like crap."

"Uncle Dante!" Daniella scolded.

"Thanks for the vote of confidence. Just what I needed before a meeting with the mayor," André said dryly.

"I've never lied, not going to start doing it now." Daniella poked him in the kidney with her pointy finger. "What?" he looked down at her.

Instead of answering, Daniella extended a hand toward André, saying, "Hi, I'm Daniella er-Brown. Dante is my uncle."

André smiled and shook her hand. "It's a pleasure to meet you, Daniella. I'm André Dear, chief of police of Cooper Springs. How are you liking the town?"

"It's fine, I guess."

Before they could go any further and possibly open up the "what's wrong with Cooper Springs" conversation or, god forbid, the "why Daniella needs a dog" one, Dante intervened.

"You've been busy lately."

Because murder was always a great topic to bring up. Dante winced. Maybe right here was the reason he was still single.

André met his gaze of chagrin. "It's always busy, but yes, it has been a bit overwhelming. No rest for any of us."

"Well," Dante said awkwardly, "we should let you get to your shopping."

"I'd rather be called out repeatedly in the middle of the night in the pouring rain when I'm out of coffee."

"Uncle Dante hates shopping too. I don't get it."

They both turned and looked at Daniella.

"Tell you what, when you get your driver's license, I'll pay you to pick up the groceries," Dante said—and meant it.

"Let me know. I might want in on the deal too."

The radio fastened to André's chest crackled to life. André sighed and rolled his eyes. "I told them I needed an hour, one

damn hour, to grab groceries, and they can't even manage that."
Abandoning his basket, Dear moved toward the exit.

"We should get those for him," Daniella said.

"You think?" Because yes, they should, but Dante wanted it to
be Dani's idea.

"It's the right thing to do. How will he be a good police officer
if he doesn't have decent food to eat?"

There was, of course, The Steam Donkey, Pizza Mart, and
whatever quasi-food the gas station carried, but a person could
only live on that for so long. Leaning down, Dante picked up the
plastic basket and set it inside the cart. Was this an excuse to see
André? Maybe, but it was also basic human kindness.

At least, that's what Dante told himself.

SEVEN

André

Unknown number: You might as well send me a grocery list. Dani and I are headed to A.

Momentarily distracted, André stared at his cell phone's screen. How the hell had Dante gotten his number? There was no one else it could be, not unless he had some very odd stalker who got his kicks from grocery lists and enjoyed driving to Aberdeen to fill them. And who also knew someone named Dani.

André: How did you get this number?

Dante: Asked the gal at the front desk. She's very nice BTW.

André was tempted to argue with Dante. Or to lie and say he'd just been to Aberdeen and his refrigerator was full of food waiting to be cooked. Truth was, the last of the yogurt had been eaten over the weekend, and he was going to have to toss out the disgusting vegetable mush in the crisper drawer before it became sentient.

He was also going to have a chat with Carol about the importance of personal information and not giving it out to random strangers.

Dante: Don't be mad at her. I flashed my badge and told her it was about a case.

André shut his eyes for just a second. He was still going to have to talk to her, but Dante used charm like a weapon and if anyone could pry information out of Carol, it would be him. His phone pinged again.

Dante: Groceries. Do you buy the same stuff all the time? If so, that's easy. Yogurt/bread/milk/granola/sandwich meat/frozen pizza?

A sigh escaped André. Yes, he did buy the same stuff all the time. Cooking for one was a pain in the ass. He'd been touched the other week when, after running into Dante and his niece at the store and being forced to abandon his basket, he'd come home and found his groceries sitting on the front porch. Not that he'd sought Dante out and thanked him for it. Fine, he'd let Dante pick up groceries. This one time.

André: Yep, sounds about right. Thanks.

It felt like Dante buying groceries for him was a slippery slope. But André had more important battles to fight than agreeing to have edible food in his house. With the Christmas holiday just a few days away, André had zero desire to make the effort to go to the store. There was always popcorn, right? He'd figure out how to pay Dante back later—this, he suspected, would be tricky.

In the meantime, he had a deputy to deal with. André couldn't force Deputy Lionel Trent to resign, but it would have made his life much easier. How the man had managed to stay on the force for over forty years was beyond the scope of André's imagination. Incompetent was just one descriptor for the older man. *Criminal* was another possibility.

Trent seemed to believe that it was his job to enforce the law. And it was. But it was also his job to protect the public. Literally, protect and serve. It hadn't taken André long to figure out that

Trent believed the public owed him and not the other way around. He greatly preferred the enforcement side.

Like many small towns, Cooper Springs still had a strong good-old-boy network, one André suspected Trent was the current president of. A friend speeding? Trent let it slide. André had noted, however, that Trent had ticketed Lizzy Harlow almost ten times. Did he think Trent was involved in her death? Truthfully, André thought Trent was too lazy for murder. And he had no evidence. Plus, Trent would know where in the county to hide a body, and in the marsh next to the old resort was not it.

The forest was much more likely.

André had spent several hours creating a spreadsheet with every ticket given by Deputy Trent—and, for comparison's sake, Deputy Cooper—in the last three years. Hours of painstaking data entry had led André to conclude that Trent gave out significantly more moving violation tickets to women and minorities. Lani did not. André had a hard time believing it was coincidence that Trent stopped more women than men and more people of color than the overwhelming White population who lived in the area.

André firmly believed the adage, "Where there's smoke, there's fire." Lionel Trent was smoking, and André needed to figure out exactly what the man was up to. He wasn't looking forward to the upcoming conversation.

A knock sounded on his door, and he glanced up at the clock. It was too early for Deputy Trent; he liked to keep André waiting, especially the last few times they'd had meetings.

"Come in."

Carol poked her head inside.

"Chief Dear, I'm afraid Deputy Trent called."

A sigh escaped him. "Let me guess. Trent is running late?"

Carol shot him a tentative smile. "Yes. Well actually, he's not going to make it. Apparently, something has come up."

"Something's come up, alright," André grumbled. "If he

bothers to call back, do your best to encourage him to make our meeting." André wasn't picking up the phone to call him. His fuse was short this afternoon.

André knew he was lucky Carol had stayed on when he'd taken the chief's position. Without her and Lani Cooper, he would be lost. Being the police chief of a small town required institutional knowledge that André was only just beginning to learn. Tip of the iceberg was an overstatement.

"Yes, sir." With a nod, Carol disappeared back down the short hallway to the tiny lobby and reception area—her domain. She also was the head dispatcher—the only dispatcher. Another problem for André to solve. But not today.

He wondered if Trent thought he was fooling André. While he didn't have hard proof for this either, André knew secondhand that Trent accepted "gifts," and his paperwork barely passed muster when he bothered to finish it. Since coming on board in Cooper Springs, André had done what he could to keep Trent on traffic duty, but the deputy had gone to the union a month ago and complained that he had seniority over Lani Cooper.

Trent did have seniority over the town's only other deputy. But, unlike Trent, Lani had the brains to do the job and wasn't shady. Trent was shady as fuck. With the murder of Lizzy Harlow and the other, much older, remains being discovered—and he couldn't forget the missing teen, Blair Cruz—Cooper Springs had trouble on its hands, and it was André's literal job to get to the bottom of it.

Was Trent somehow involved in the missing and murdered?

André didn't think the sixty-something deputy had it in him. He was more of a "skim it off the top and hope no one notices" kind of person, maybe skip handing out a ticket but get a free coffee next time he was at the gas station. Although he did drive a late model Dodge Charger, definitely not something a small-town cop could normally afford. All André had to do was think about the Green River Killer. He'd operated right under the noses of the police and his coworkers for decades. How many lives might have been saved if someone had just asked the right questions in the nineties?

His cell phone buzzed again, distracting André from his unpleasant meanderings.

Dante: There's been a run on yogurt. All that's left is eggnog flavor.

André gagged a little and felt his stomach do a little *no way* twist. Over twenty years since he'd gotten drunk on the stuff, and he still couldn't stand the smell of eggnog.

A: No. Cottage cheese?

D: Are you asking or telling?

André rolled his eyes up to the ceiling, noting that an industrious spider had spun a web in one corner. He'd have to ask Carol where the broom was.

A: Cottage cheese. Not asking.

D: Are you sure? That shit has a weird flavor.

A: Just. yes.

D: No frozen pizza.

A: They don't have any?

If the store was out of frozen pizza, the world was probably coming to an end. Had André missed the memo?

D: They do. It's also shit. Mine is better.

André blinked. What was this conversation about? Was Dante offering to make him pizza? No. They hadn't seen each other except in passing since that time Dante had stopped by back in October. André had made sure of that. There was no way he and Dante were picking up where they left off. October had been a moment of weakness.

A: All I need is a few Hot Pockets, something that won't go bad if I forget about it.

There was no immediate reply. André set his phone down again and eyed the spider settled in the center of its web. On general principle, André didn't much like spiders. It was the eight legs and creepy-crawly aspect that got to him. This one seemed content to stay as far away from André as it could get.

"Stay where I can see you and I'll leave you alone," he warned the arachnid, refocusing on his project.

Not too much later, Carol stuck her head in to say she was heading to lunch.

"Ned hasn't been by yet, just so he doesn't scare you when he shows up."

"Thanks for the heads-up."

Ned Barker was the postman for the area. He'd unintentionally scared the crap out of André early on, surprising him in the breakroom when André had thought the station was empty. Now Carol never forgot to let André know if the mail had been delivered or not.

Lionel Trent rolled in around midafternoon, hitching up his slacks and pushing out his chest in an attempt—André assumed —to appear intimidating. He didn't bother to take off his hat or his jacket, either.

"Sorry, boss." Not sounding or appearing sorry. "I had a family issue come up that I needed to help out with."

André hadn't been aware Lionel had any family living in the area. As far as he knew, Lionel had been married at one time, but they'd divorced a decade ago. His ex-wife had moved out of town to Morton or Vader. André made a mental note to ask Carol about Trent's family.

"I hope everything is okay."

"It'll be fine," Lionel replied dismissively.

"Have a seat, Lionel."

Lionel blinked, his gaze darting to the chair and then back to André. "I should relieve Deputy Cooper, sir."

"This won't take us long," André said with a toothy smile that did not reach his eyes.

Deputy Trent stomped out of André's office five minutes later and took a right turn toward the parking lot at the back of the building. He was not pleased about being sent to a Cultural Sensitivity and Bias Training workshop, and André didn't expect the class to make much of a difference. But down the road, when Lionel Trent failed to change his way of policing and was released from the force, André would be able to say he'd tried.

~

By the time he arrived home, André had completely forgotten about the text exchange with Dante. He was beyond exhausted. For a minute or so, he sat behind the wheel of his trusty Jeep and eyed his dark and presumably cold house.

It was very much the outlier on the block. Holiday decorations did not cover every inch of the exterior. No tree. No lights inside. Nothing. His lot was a void in a galaxy of blinding, colorful lights.

The clock on the dashboard told him there was still time to grab something to eat at The Steam Donkey but that Pizza Mart was closed already. His stomach rumbled in complaint, but his fingers made the decision for him, unlocking and pushing the car door open. He did not want to be that pathetic single man who ate at the diner most nights, sad and alone in a booth with a stained plastic red-checkered tablecloth, always ordering the roast beef sandwich and a slice of pie. That way madness lay.

He opened the door and climbed out.

As he approached his porch, André abruptly remembered Dante's texts and a jolt of hope shot through his chest. He might not have to eat popcorn for dinner after all. But the closer he got up the walkway, the more the spark of hope faded. There were no grocery bags waiting by the door. Dante had obviously come to his senses and decided André could fend for himself.

"Stupid André. What were you thinking?" he muttered as he dug in his pocket for the house keys.

Fine. That was fine. He didn't want to get used to Dante's presence in town anyway. Soon enough, he'd be gone again.

Although, a little voice said, *would he?* With a niece to look after? André pushed the thought aside.

"You're a grown adult, André. Act like it."

Maybe a good start would be not talking to himself on the front porch.

His front door opened directly into the living room, which ran the width of the house. At one end of the room was a quasi-eating space, and the other side was taken up by the couch and TV. Reaching to the right, André flipped on the overhead light and then shrugged out of his damp raincoat, hanging it on the coatrack next to the entrance. Then he crossed over to the couch and sat down, tugging his heavy police-issue footwear off his feet.

"Jesus, that feels good."

His stomach growled, reminding André that instant noodles eight hours ago were not enough to hold body and soul together for long.

With a groan, he heaved himself up again and headed into his small but well-designed kitchen to the refrigerator. Surely, the sentient vegetables wouldn't attack.

He blinked against the glare of the light from inside the fridge, shut the door, then opened it again. The contents absolutely had not been there that morning: a carton of milk, a small container of cottage cheese, a deli bag of sliced ham, and another of roast beef.

"What the fuck?"

The groceries he had not put there didn't reply.

"What the fuck," he repeated as he slammed the door shut and went in search of his cell phone.

A: What the fuck.

There wasn't an immediate response to his text. André glared at the screen as if, by willpower alone, he could force Dante to answer. To explain why he'd broken into André's house and left groceries in his refrigerator. André made a mental note to have a security company come out and set up a system. He'd never felt the need for one before because he'd lived in an apartment building. Admittedly, he'd never worried about someone breaking in and leaving things instead of taking them, either.

"This is fucking ridiculous," André muttered.

Five minutes later, there was still no response, and André did something he'd restrained himself from doing months ago. He sat down on the couch, opened his laptop, and searched for Dante's address. He hadn't wanted to know where the man lived—or rather, he had, but since André had left Portland to start a new life, it had seemed a poor decision to chase down someone from his old one.

He typed in Dante Castone and pressed Enter. There were no results, which wasn't really a surprise. Dante was not publicly listed as living anywhere in or around Cooper Springs. But André knew the man lived in town—he'd said his niece went to the high school.

Narrowing his eyes, André stared out the window across from him, gazing at nothing but the darkness, forcing his brain to think. At the grocery store that day, the niece had introduced herself as Daniella Brown.

With shaking fingers, André typed in Dante Brown. Surely the man got mail or had a landline, or something.

No results.

André stared out the window a bit longer before another thought struck him. Before he'd left that morning in October, Dante had said his sister had been killed, but not how. André wasn't a U.S. Marshal with access to privileged information anymore. But he had friends who were, and they owed him.

Just as he was picking up his phone to call in that favor, there was a knock on his door. Slamming the lid of his laptop shut, he stepped across the room and opened the door, not bothering to look through the peephole. He knew exactly who was waiting on the other side.

Dante and Daniella were illuminated under the dim light

thrown off by the porch bulb. Dante had a slightly apologetic expression on his face and held something in his hands. Daniella had her hands wrapped around a foil-covered bowl.

"Evening," Dante said. "We thought we'd just come over and save the trouble of texting."

The scent of something absolutely delicious wafted up from the tray Dante held. André's stomach growled again, and his mouth started to water.

Dante quirked a dark eyebrow. "Can we come in?"

"As if you haven't been in already," André said grimly, trying to hold on to his anger as he opened the door wider and stepped back to allow them inside.

"As if you'd have said yes if I offered to make you dinner," Dante pointed out. "This is our dinner too. We're merely including you."

André was too hungry to protest. He'd do that later. And Dante was infuriatingly correct. He would never have said yes to dinner.

"Let me clear off the table."

The dining table was covered with mail André hadn't opened, paperwork that needed filling out, and a few banker's boxes packed with some cold cases he'd been going through at home because his office was too damn small. André usually ate sitting on the couch or standing at the kitchen counter. Quickly, he piled the boxes in a corner, promising himself he'd go through them soon.

Minutes later, the three of them were seated around the round oak table. Dante took the lid off the tray, revealing some kind of pasta dish. The bowl Daniella had brought in held a simple green salad.

"Eat," commanded Dante as he scooped pasta onto the plates he'd brought in from the kitchen.

"Not going to argue," André replied, picking up his fork and stabbing at the noodles.

"That's a first," Dante mumbled under his breath, not so quiet that Daniella didn't hear him though. She bit her lip and shot André a small grin as she glanced between the two of them.

The pasta was incredible. Unashamed, André helped himself to seconds. Who knew when his next decent meal would be? They didn't talk much; André was too busy shoveling food into his mouth while Dante and Daniella discussed school starting up again and what her class schedule was going to be like. Listening to them, André wondered what the two would do for Christmas. He had volunteered to cover the station seeing as how he had no relatives to visit.

"Do you like dogs, Chief Dear?"

André breathed in all wrong, coughed, and nearly choked on his last bite of pasta. Reaching over, Dante pounded him between the shoulder blades.

When he could breathe again and had wiped the tears from his eyes, André rasped, "Just André here, no need to call me chief."

"Okay," she said, her cheeks a little flushed. "Do you like dogs?"

"Daniella," Dante said, his tone warning.

"Zio, I'm just asking."

"I know exactly what you are asking, *topolina*."

"I do like dogs," André interjected, assuming *topolina* was an endearment of some kind. "But my work schedule would be very hard on a pet. It's somewhat of a shame because there's a big yard out back."

"Enough about dogs or pets of any kind," Dante said darkly. "We should get home, Daniella. The chief needs his beauty sleep. Let's get the table cleared and dishes taken care of."

Ten minutes later, André stood at the door, bemused as fuck. He hadn't even remembered to tell Dante off for breaking into his house and leaving groceries. Nope. Instead, he'd wolfed down the food the small family had brought over and listened to the uncle and niece chat about their lives. It had felt homelike, something André was unfamiliar with in his adult life. And before that too, if he was being truthful.

He stood watching the red lights of Dante's car disappear down the street.

"I still don't know where the asshole lives," he said with an irritated snort.

As he was shutting the front door, another car, this one a black late model SUV, started down the block, passing slowly in front of his house. Out of habit, André stood to the side and watched it from his front window. He hadn't survived almost two decades as a marshal by being careless.

The dark night and lack of streetlights made it impossible to see the driver or if there were any passengers. But he didn't recognize the vehicle and wasn't shocked to note that the license plate was partially obscured.

Were they looking for André or Dante? Or was his overactive imagination making monsters out of thin air? He twitched the curtain closed and made sure both his front and back doors were secured as he got ready for bed.

After the day he'd had, André should have been asleep in minutes. Instead, he lay there staring at the ceiling, thinking about Dante Castone and his niece, and wondering what the hell was going on in Cooper Springs.

EIGHT

Dante

The Christmas holiday hurt.

Dante had expected it to be painful. But maybe not sticking a needle in his eye painful.

It was Dani's first major holiday without Simone, and his as well. As the older sibling, Simone had always been there for Dante. Everything fucking sucked and Dante's skill set didn't exactly include helping teenagers with their grief. He was an action rather than words kind of person, and he had the scars to prove it.

As luck would have it, Dani's friend Romy invited them over for a midafternoon meal, thus saving them from sitting around the crappy house staring at each other for too long. They hadn't even gotten a tree because Dani insisted she didn't want one and Dante hadn't had it in him to force the issue. Maybe next year.

Had Dante known the meal would be held at Vincent Barone's boyfriend's house and attended by no less than six other adults and three dogs, he might have tried to come up with a reason why they couldn't attend.

On the other hand, seeing Dani light up around her friend and those damn dogs was a gift Dante would never turn down. This was the only explanation for why he and Dani were headed to the shelter on New Year's Eve eve to take a look at the available dogs.

"We're just looking," he said for the hundredth time. "We not coming home with a dog today."

"Romy said the shelter makes you wait anyway, so they can do background checks."

Dante quickly glanced at nis niece. Her fingers were restlessly tapping her thigh as she looked out through the windshield.

"Correct," Dante said, directing his attention back to the roadway.

"It's to keep creeps from adopting animals."

"That is true. I'm all for background checks." If and when Dani ever started dating, Dante would be doing a deep dive on anyone she brought home. Was that an invasion of her privacy? Undoubtedly. Would he likely do it anyway? Damn straight he would.

"Thank you for taking me, Zio."

"Quit piling on the Zio crap," he teased.

Was adopting a dog the wrong thing to do? Most likely, he would end up taking care of it. That was what happened. Kids got excited and when the glow wore off, the parent—or guardian, in his case—was left with the begged-for pet. Dante recalled being eight and thinking he wanted a hamster. Thankfully, no one had paid any attention to him. Being the youngest in a large, extended family had been a blessing and a curse. The pet rock had been his next choice and a good one until Lu had gotten his hands on it.

They turned into the gravel drive that led to the shelter. The building it was housed in dated from the 1980s and looked depressing as fuck. From where they were in the parking lot, they could hear dogs barking and at least one baying.

Please, he thought, *not a hound*.

"Poor things, they sound so sad," Dani said. "They just want their own homes."

Dante rolled his eyes in a decidedly almost-sixteen-year-old-girl fashion.

"You've made your point. Let's go."

A couple of days after their trip to the pound, Dante was keeping an eye out the front window while Dani threw a bright orange, very bougie—and very bouncy—dog toy for Luna. The sound of Dani's cajoling laughter and Luna's excited, demanding barks did something squishy to Dante's heart. Or maybe it was just heartburn.

"I'll keep her safe, Simone," he promised his dead sister for the thousandth time since August.

The dog, Luna, was a Shepard mix of some kind—active, agile, and smart. She and Dani had bonded in minutes. She'd need a bigger yard eventually, but Dante couldn't think about that until after the trial.

Almost as if the universe was eavesdropping on his thoughts, Dante's phone rang. He checked the screen. *Chris Hatch.*

"Hatch," Dante said after pressing Accept.

"Castone." Chris's greeting was raspy.

"You sound like shit. Why are you calling?"

"Got a cold. General update and just checking in on you. There's been whispering about the Campos organization."

A growl rolled up inside Dante's chest. Outside, Luna leaped up and grabbed the bouncy ball out of the air and Dani laughed. Dante ground his teeth.

"Maybe it's just gossip. But Aldo might be upping efforts to get that get out of jail free card. The two suspects in Simone's murder were found." Dante perked up. Maybe this shit show was over. Hatch continued, "Before you get excited—dead. Very dead. As in, it took a while for them to be identified and one is a nobody. Alonso Campos is in the wind. We had eyes on him, but he's disappeared. Which frankly is a pain in my ass."

That was unfortunate. Dante wondered who was getting demoted over that.

"Dante." Hatch's tone seemed wary as he continued. "Aldo told his lawyer to pass along his condolences to you. He is 'sending his thoughts and prayers,' to be exact."

Dante stiffened at the words. Aldo Compos was a psychopath. He wanted out of federal detention and would do everything he could to make it so.

"That's the real reason you're calling me."

"The higher-ups would like you to check with Daniella one last time. Maybe she'll have remembered something new."

Dante wondered if he should remind his ex-boss that there were actual qualified homicide detectives on his sister's case. On the other hand, this was his sister, his niece's mother, and he wanted justice.

"In my opinion, he's stirring the pot," continued Hatch. "And not only is he good at it, but he also has his unhinged little brother on the outside keeping him updated. He's not planning on going to prison."

"He's already in prison."

"You know what I mean. Staying there."

"Why did you really call? Just to tell me a psychopath is still after my niece?"

"Stay vigilant, Castone. Don't let your guard down. I really wish you'd gone WITSEC." Another pause. "If you need anything, let me know."

Dante glanced back out the window. Dani was bending over Luna, petting her and presumably telling the dog what a good girl she was. Not wanting to add to her trauma, they hadn't talked about what had happened that night since he'd picked her up from Hatch's office. Was it possible Dani knew something more without realizing it was important? Possible, but not probable.

Dante knew kids heard shit they shouldn't, but Simone had been tight-lipped. Still, they needed to talk again and sooner rather than later.

"Fuck."

"Keep her safe, Castone."

"With my life."

Hatch clicked off and Dante moved closer to the window. He needed to call Dani inside but didn't look forward to the laughter and joy fading from her expression. A few houses away, a nondescript gray sedan parked against the curb caught Dante's attention. He'd never noticed it before. He didn't like it.

Without conscious thought, he stepped forward and yanked the front door open.

"Dani!" he bellowed.

His niece's attention jerked from the dog to him. Dante must not have been as good as he thought at hiding his feelings. Dani's face paled as she grabbed Luna's collar, and they ran toward him and into the house.

"Sorry, honey," Dante said, wrapping his arms around his trembling niece. "I didn't mean to scare you."

"What happened?" she asked.

Luna seemed to sense that Dani and Dante were upset. She leaned hard into their legs as if she was trying to hold them up or include herself in their hug.

"Nothing."

"Zio." Dani's warning tone sounded remarkably like her mother's.

Squeezing her tighter, Dante said. "My old boss, Hatch, just called."

"Oh," she said in a near whisper.

Dante let a sigh slip out. "We need to talk more about what happened the night Simone died." And maybe about other times as well, but they'd cross that bridge when they came to it.

"I've told you everything," Dani protested. Dante could tell she didn't want to talk, to remember what had happened. He didn't either.

"I know you have, topolina. But sometimes things that seem unimportant or small when the shit is flying around turn out to be a big deal. Honestly, I've been putting it off, but we can't any longer."

And maybe he needed to come clean with the chief of police as to the real reason he and Dani were in Cooper Springs. Fuck. Not *maybe*. They needed to have a conversation. André deserved to know that trouble could be coming to town.

More trouble.

And Dante knew André was going to be pissed that they hadn't gone into witness protection. Well, too late now.

"One last time, let's go over what happened."

Dani stared at him, pressing her lips together and narrowing her eyes. Times like this she looked so much like Simone.

"Please?"

She relented and started to recount the worst night of her life, quickly and without emotion, obviously wanting to get through the ordeal as soon as possible.

"It was nighttime. I was coming downstairs to ask a question, and Mom was opening the door. The man just... shot her. I froze, then he looked around and up to where I was. He lifted the gun up and I thought he was going to shoot me too, but the person on the sidewalk said something and scared them away."

"There was nothing about the man? No tattoos or nose rings? No squinty eye? A boil?"

She shook her head. "Nothing more than what I already said. He had a cap pulled down low and all I could see were his eyes and mouth. It was dark."

"And your mom never talked to you about her work?" Dante asked, knowing what the answer would be.

"No, never. I knew she was a prosecutor, but I never knew what cases she was working on. She said it wasn't fair to talk to me about them. If I accidentally said something to a friend and it got out, her case could be... compromised. That was the word Mom used."

"She was right. Your mom was the smartest person I've ever known."

He hugged his precious niece one last time before releasing her and rising to his feet. "I may not be a genius, but I'll keep you safe and so will Luna."

"Who's going to keep you safe, Zio?" Dani asked.

"Don't you worry, topolina. I've got mad skills."

The expression in Dani's brown eyes told him she was skeptical but also wasn't going to press the issue—yet. Luna nuzzled her hand, presumably looking for a treat, and while Dani was distracted, Dante peered out the window again. The sedan was gone.

All hell broke loose a few days later, just before Dani went back to school again.

On New Year's Day, Nick Waugh and Martin Purdy, the new owner of Cooper Springs Resort, found a cache of bones along one of the trails behind town. They'd been confirmed as human.

Cooper Springs was buzzing—and not in a good way.

"Please, Zio?"

Dante stared at his niece. Again? Was she batting her eyes? He was barely holding himself together between the news Hatch had dropped on him about Aldo Campos and the swirling rumors about the bones that he'd been privy to when he'd filled his car up with gas that morning. And she wanted to go hang out with friends?

"You want to go to Pizza Mart?" he asked as if he hadn't heard clearly.

Dani nodded. "To hang out with Romy."

"I'm not letting you go alone."

He was still upset by Hatch's call and the discovery of yet *more* remains made him fucking twitchy. Not to mention that fucking gray sedan. Had the driver been watching him? Was it his imagination working overtime? Something nasty was going on in Cooper Springs, and he did not like it one bit. If he wasn't careful, though, Dani would pick up on his barely controlled emotions. He consciously took a deep breath and did his best to relax his shoulders.

"Okay," she agreed simply, not fooled by his deep breathing techniques. Apparently, he was not as good at hiding his feelings as he'd thought. "But maybe you can sit somewhere else?"

As if he wanted to know what the teenaged population of Cooper Springs was talking about. Actually, he already knew. It was probably the remains.

And fucking dammit, he'd hoped she would be deterred by his insistence on being a chaperone.

Dani, Romy, and two other kids were sitting in a booth on the other side of the restaurant. Dante was nursing a watery Coke and attempting to blend into the background. He suspected he was failing because every time the door opened, he felt new eyes on him.

Eventually, someone he recognized came in. Vincent Barone. Vincent gave his kid a chin nod and headed for Dante's table, not asking permission before he pulled out a chair and sat down across from him.

"Happy New Year," Vincent said with an irritating smile, making himself as comfortable as was possible in the too-small plastic chairs.

"No offense," Dante said, sitting back in his seat and crossing his arms over his chest, "but what are you doing here?"

Vincent smiled again and leaned onto the table. "Romy texted and asked me to come distract you. Apparently, you're scaring people."

"And you had nothing better to do?"

"Nope, not really." He shook his head. "High school teacher, remember?"

Right. "Thanks again for having us on Christmas, and Happy New Year." He wasn't a monster; he could be social. Maybe.

"No prob. So, what are you doing here, looking scary?"

Dante debated what he should or could tell Vincent. The man wasn't an idiot. He knew something was up. What normal adult person would hang out in Pizza Mart?

"The news." Dante nodded in the direction of the forest. "It's got me on edge."

Vincent sat forward. "Me too. All of us, really. It sounds like the bones've been there a while, but damn, it makes me want to lock Romy inside the house and throw away the key."

"That's about where I am."

But more like he wanted to wrap Dani in cotton and lock her in a fortress. Tomato, tahmahtoe.

"Are you in law enforcement?" Vincent abruptly asked.

"Not anymore. Why?"

"You have that look about you. Law enforcement or motor-cycle gang."

Reluctantly, Dante chuckled. Barone was too close on both accounts, considering his last undercover assignment *had* been infiltrating that OMC. That life was definitely over now.

"I do my best to tone it down, but I was a LEO for a long time. It doesn't just go away."

Vincent glanced at Dante's nearly finished Coke. "You want another one of those, or do you want to leave the teens here and go have a quick beer at the Donkey? They'll be fine for an hour and believe me, the food at the pub is more to our taste."

Dante debated refusing. But Dani would be going back to

school, and he couldn't follow her everywhere. Might as well start practicing now.

Fucking hell.

"Sure, sounds good."

Dani tried to hide her smile when Dante told her he'd be up the street, but she wasn't quite successful.

"Just," he said, glancing around the table to include the other kids, "be mindful. And text me when you're ready to go home."

They claimed an empty table opposite the door. The pub wasn't packed—a lot of folks were probably trying to hold to their New Year's resolutions, but there were folks taking up quite a few of the booths and sitting on the stools along the bar anyway.

"Thanks," Dante said as he sat down again. "I guess I get a little overprotective."

Vincent grinned. "Believe me when I tell you how much I understand. Romy tests my every nerve. She just doesn't understand how scary the world is. I dread the day she graduates from high school."

Dani'd already had a lesson in how shitty the world was, but that didn't stop Dante from worrying.

"You two are close though, right?"

It had seemed like they got along at the holiday dinner. Dante had learned that Barone was bi and had a boyfriend, and Romy seemed fine with the whole situation.

"We are." Vincent nodded. "It's been the two of us for a while now. Still, she's going to spread her wings wide, and soon. It scares the crap out of me."

The bartender stopped by, and they each ordered a beer. Dante had only been Dani's guardian for four months, but he knew exactly how Vincent felt. How had Simone managed this whole parenting thing?

As that grim thought crossed his mind, the front door opened, and Dante immediately recognized André Dear's silhouette. His heart skipped a beat, as if he was a teenager seeing his first crush. The man paused for a moment, probably to let his eyes adjust to the dim lighting. Dante could almost feel André's glance when it landed on him.

Vincent turned to see what had caught his attention and, before Dante could stop him, raised his hand and waved André over.

"André! Have a seat. We just got here."

Did he imagine a slight hesitation before André headed in their direction? Fuck if he knew. Vincent pulled out the chair beside him and André's gaze met Dante's as he sat down. His heart began to beat faster.

"Been a rough couple of days for you, hasn't it?" Vincent said when André was comfortable.

"That's one way of putting it."

Dante eyed André, taking in his appearance. After years in law enforcement, he was probably good at hiding how he felt, but Dante could tell he was exhausted. There were shadows under his eyes, and he hadn't shaved. Dante could see the sexy glint of silver in his scruff spark under the pub's lighting.

"It doesn't help that everyone in town has decided to become a backyard detective. Folks have been calling the station with all sorts of tips." André made finger quotes around the word tips. "Some of it could be helpful—like the fact that there seems to have been disappearances going back to the seventies—but most of it is probably useless, and Carol is not equipped to run a hotline." He eyed them. "Do I have to tell you two not to spread this around?"

He and Vincent both shook their heads.

"Do you have the budget to hire someone to just take the calls?" Dante asked.

André frowned. "No, but the mayor wants to meet with me. I'm hoping that means she's wrangled money from somewhere.

None of my staff has the experience for this type of investigation."

"There's only one way to get it," Dante pointed out. He wanted to offer to help. He knew his way around police reports.

André scowled. "My staff of two deputies is fifty percent useless." His eyes widened as he glanced around again. "Shit. Don't repeat that either. The union is already on me."

"Deputy Trent causing issues again?" Vincent was scowling now.

"Maybe."

"We all know it's not Lani Cooper. Lionel Trent has never been a good cop." André and Dante both stared at him, waiting for Vincent to clarify. "Xavier was jumped as a teen, and yeah, Xavier was trouble back in the day, but this was a clear case of bashing and Trent was the investigating officer. He did nothing."

"Fuck," André growled. "But sadly, I am not surprised."

Dante shook his head. He didn't know this Trent character, but the truth was that there were people who just shouldn't be in law enforcement.

The bartender returned with Dante's and Vincent's beers. "Sorry this took so long," he said. "What can I get you, Chief?"

"I'm off duty for the rest of the day, fingers crossed. A beer sounds good. Thanks, Garth."

Garth headed back to the taps and the three men were quiet for a bit while Dante and Vincent each took a sip of beer. Dante didn't know what the other two were thinking about, but he would bet Vincent wasn't thinking about how to get André alone, make sure he got something to eat, and then maybe strip his clothes off and help him relax.

"Dante?"

Shit. "What?"

"Did you get a dog?" André repeated.

"How did you know?"

André shrugged. "I figure that niece of yours has you wrapped around her little finger."

Dante rolled his eyes. "We went to the shelter a few days ago. The dog's name is Luna."

The server brought André's beer over and left again, leaving them to a conversation that felt slightly stilted and awkward. Dante wanted André to himself so he could ask what he'd wanted to since the man walked in.

Are you okay?

As Dante watched André sip his lager, a realization hit him. He must have unintentionally made some kind of sound because both Vincent and André were looking at him.

"Everything alright?" Vincent asked.

"Fine, fine." Dante nodded, gripping his half-empty pint glass. "Just wondering if I remembered to turn off the coffee pot." Fucking not at all fine.

Both men nodded at his ridiculous excuse and Dante slid a glance at André. Did his questioning gaze linger on him a little bit longer?

Why had it taken *this* encounter to realize that he and André Dear had never had a real conversation? They'd met in a bar, over a year ago now, and had gone home together. Since then, their limited conversations had occurred on the way to sex or, more rarely, after it. In his defense, being undercover for years on different assignments for the DEA meant Dante wasn't used to talking. Talking got a person in deep trouble.

No wonder André didn't trust him. Dante wouldn't trust himself either. Had he really thought that André would just fall into his arms? No, he hadn't. But obviously, he was going to have to up his game. And while being LGBTQA+ in Cooper Springs didn't seem to be an issue, was André even out?

A few patrons eyed their table and slowed as they passed by, obviously considering approaching Chief Dear. Dante shot them his best stink eye and they found something else of interest to focus on.

Vincent kept the conversation going by bringing up the weather—a legitimate topic considering a winter storm was in the forecast and folks were battening down the hatches. Dante made a mental note to get the ladder out of the garage and check the gutters. Even if he wanted André to himself, he was glad Vincent had invited him for a beer. After years undercover and his general upbringing, it was always hard to make real friends.

Dante had almost finished his drink when Dani texted that she was ready to go home. Throwing back the last sip, he set the pint glass back down on the table.

"I've got to go, Uncle Duty calls."

And more importantly, he needed some quiet space to figure out exactly what his plan was when it came to André Dear.

NINE

André

"Thank you, Chief, for not fighting me on this."

"We need all the help we can get, Mayor Moore. I'm not ashamed to admit it."

Mayor Roslyn Moore pressed her lips together in a grim line and met his gaze. They both knew a capital-S shitstorm was about to hit Cooper Springs.

So far, the story about the newest remains had only been picked up by a local blogger, but soon enough, state and national news would be crawling all over like flies on crap. The local gossips would be fighting to line up at the vans and share their versions of something they knew absolutely nothing about. André wanted to put them all under house arrest. But he couldn't.

Dammit.

Regardless, he exited the mayor's office a tad bemused but also ever so slightly more hopeful than he had been before he'd gone in. Maybe they'd solve this case. When he'd met Roslyn Moore during his interview, she'd seemed efficient and dedicated to the job she was elected for—running Cooper Springs. He was glad his impression wasn't wrong. Moore was in her sixties, but there were no signs she was slowing down, and now she'd come up with resources that brought them even closer to discovering who the remains belonged to.

This afternoon André had learned that her son, Ethan Moore, was a top forensic anthropologist connected to West Coast Forensics. WCF was well-known, well-respected, and privately owned by ex-LEOs. André had met one of the owners, Kimball Frye, at a conference once and been impressed by his professional knowledge.

Now Ethan Moore was on his way to town to help with the investigation into the remains Nick Waugh and Martin Purdy had found. André hoped that, even if they were never able to catch the person or people who'd buried at least two people up on the mountain and possibly more, the remains might at least be identified. Then maybe there would be closure for family and friends waiting to hear from a loved one. In André's opinion, it was never too late to learn the truth.

André paused in the empty lobby to stare at the etched-glass door in disgust. To no one, he said, "Damn glad I drove. Cats and dogs have nothing on this." It was January, but did it have to be quite so miserable? Quite so wet? He didn't remember Portland being this bad.

With a put-upon sigh, he pushed the door open and hurried to the police cruiser parked directly at the curb. The joys of small-town living.

His pleasant mood was destroyed—obliterated—when he arrived back at the station.

"Chief," Carol said as he shut the door firmly behind him, "may I have a word?"

"Of course, Carol. Anytime."

He stopped at her desk, assuming his dispatcher was going to tell him that Lionel Trent was AWOL again, or that Hardy Phinney and Eustis Kurr were at each other's throats. They seemed to have buried the hatchet recently, but maybe their feud went in cycles?

His stomach sank. It couldn't be more remains, could it?

"In your office?" she asked.

His stomach twisting into knots, André led the way back to his tiny—but bigger than anyone else's—office. It was just large enough for an ancient filing cabinet that was too heavy for anyone to move, his metal desk that was probably from the fifties, his chair that thankfully wasn't, and two exceedingly hard plastic chairs for visitors. They didn't tend to stay long. He especially enjoyed his view of the holding cells when his door was open.

"What's up?" he asked as he took off his dripping jacket and hung it up. Luckily, the flooring was tile although it was going to be slippery as snot now.

Carol didn't answer immediately, which had him glance at her again. She seemed ill at ease.

"Sit down," he said. "Has something happened? Is it Trent?" Dammit, he needed to quit putting Trent at the bottom of his to-do list. With everything going on, the Trent issue was the last thing on his mind. The truth was that he just wanted Lionel Trent to go away but that wasn't going to happen.

Carol sat down on the edge of a plastic chair. André sat as well, eyeing his dispatcher.

"No, it's not Deputy Trent. I... Well, there's no other way to do this." She was wringing her hands, twisting her fingers together. Finally, she looked at him. "I'm retiring."

He stared at the most valuable non-law enforcement officer on his staff. "You're what?"

"Retiring," she repeated, firmly this time. "I'm staying through the end of the month though."

"Retiring?" he repeated as if he had a hearing issue.

"Yes. I am sorry, I know it's bad timing. But is there ever really a good time?"

André did his best to gather his thoughts. Carol was leaving—and what? Who would he find to take her place?

"I know you must be concerned about the position being open," Carol continued. "I might have been overstepping a bit, but I've reached out to someone I think will be perfect for the role. Obviously, I can't officially hire him, but I don't think you'll find anyone else who will be more dedicated to the role. And he won't retire on you."

She looked at André expectantly, as if waiting for him to ask who she had in mind. Of course, he'd hire whoever she thought was best.

"Of course," he said. "If you think this person is best and they want the job, then let's get it taken care of. What's their name?"

"Nicholas Waugh."

André blinked at Carol, barely resisting the urge to stick his finger in one ear and check if there was wax build-up.

"Nick Waugh," he said flatly.

"Yes. As I said, I've already reached out to him to see if there's an interest." Carol leaned forward and the plastic chair made a popping sound. "I've known Nick a long time." She paused to choose her next words. "He can be a bit prickly."

Fucking understatement.

"But he has a good heart and good instincts. As much as he grumbles, Nick cares about Cooper Springs. And a bonus is that he lives close by."

Cooper Springs Resort was across the highway and about a quarter mile north of the station. It was convenient. But was Nick Waugh—grouchy, socially challenged, marginally competent chainsaw artist—the right person for the job?

"Somehow, I don't think I have much choice here."

"Oh, you do, of course. I think Deputy Trent has a cousin who is unemployed."

André narrowed his eyes at his senior dispatcher. "You play a wicked game, Carol."

She smiled and straightened her back, clearly knowing she'd achieved a checkmate.

Carol stood up, automatically smoothing her skirt. "I'll let Nick know you want to speak with him before everything is official."

André watched her leave his office and wondered what else the day had in store for him. Probably it was a phalanx of news vans. He and the mayor had already discussed making a statement, but that would happen tomorrow after Ethan Moore arrived.

The rest of the day felt like he was in the eye of a hurricane. André spent it at his desk doing his best to get through the stack of paperwork he'd been avoiding, the high point being when he managed to find a few dollars left in the budget to send Deputies Cooper and Trent to a basic course on evidence collection. He was constantly shocked at how little training his deputies had, yet they were expected to be professionals.

Things were happening outside his office, he knew. But nothing that directly affected him—because Carol would have said something—or the station, or the new open cases that were about to change everything. Sometime around five, Carol poked her head in and said she was going home but had the pager with her.

"Ned Barker hasn't been by yet, FYI. And Nick said he can come in next week to talk to you and start training if you give him the thumbs-up. He and Martin are picking up some equipment for the cabins tomorrow."

André mumbled a response that had Carol nodding and disappearing, and soon enough, he was the only one in the building. Was he really hiring Nick Waugh for the dispatch position? Apparently so.

What was he going to do without Carol to run everything? He

had no idea. With that thought, he dove back into the shrinking stack of paperwork, bribing himself with the promise of dinner at the Donkey. It was chili night, he remembered. The thought of Magnus's chili and cornbread had him refocusing on the work in front of him.

Minutes after Carol departed, Ned Barker showed up.

"Here's the mail, Chief," he announced in an irritatingly cheerful manner. Like the mail delivery was the highlight of André's day. Today Ned's long gray hair was pulled back into a ponytail, and he had a hat jammed on his head.

"Thank you," said André, holding out his hand for that day's stack. He was constantly surprised by just how much mail the station received.

"There's weather out there for sure. Wind is up. It's going to get nasty around here. But you know, the mail must go through."

Nodding, André began flipping through the stack of envelopes, hoping to encourage Ned to leave. The man was known to talk, but Carol usually protected André from him.

"Well, I guess I should get going. You must be busy."

"Have a good evening, Ned."

"You too. 'Neither rain, nor snow, nor sleet, nor hail shall keep the postmen from their appointed rounds,'" Ned quoted as he slowly made his way out of André's office.

André breathed a sigh of relief when he heard the front door close. He even got up from behind his desk and strolled out to the lobby, making sure Ned was gone. He couldn't put his finger on what it was about Ned that bothered him. Was it the odd, small-town hokey way he had of speaking? Or maybe it was just André. He was swamped and stressed. Everything bothered him.

Would he have been more aware of his surroundings when he left the station an hour or so later if he hadn't spent the afternoon in a bureaucratic fever dream?

Likely not.

The shot took André completely by surprise. Not that he hadn't been shot at before, but not since leaving the Marshals Service. In fact, it wasn't until the second thunk against the cement facia of the police station caused an errant chip to fly off and slice his cheek that he comprehended what was happening.

Finally reacting, André threw himself to the ground and automatically scrabbled for his radio, but he didn't hit the button, not wanting to alert the shooter to his location. Heart pounding, he waited for the next shot. It never came. His heart skittered against his ribs as blood dripped down his injured cheek.

What the fuck was happening?

The sun had set hours ago, and the streetlights around the parking lot had kept André from seeing any flash of gunfire. He thought the shot had come from across the back of the parking lot but wasn't sure.

As he lay as still and flat as possible, partially submerged in a mud puddle with freezing cold water seeping through his clothing, André contemplated his life choices. At this very moment, he regretted them. After a few minutes passed and no more shots came, he risked the radio.

"It's fine," André said irritably. "It's just a scratch. I don't need to go to the ER, much less get in an ambulance."

Lani Cooper stared at him, hands on her hips. She'd arrived just minutes after André called. Deputy Trent was "on his way."

"Sir—"

"I hate being called sir. If you keep it up, I'm going to ma'am you."

Lani scowled. "How can you joke in a situation like this? Someone shot at you!"

André shrugged. "Not the first time it's happened to me. Admittedly, I didn't expect it to happen in Cooper Springs, but maybe I should have." He'd briefly wondered if the shooter had been Trent. Had the deputy resorted to violence? Did he hate André that much?

He'd surprised Trent in his office a week ago; had he discovered André's notes on his lack of improvement? Lionel had made some excuse about needing a secure internet connection which could, unfortunately, have been true.

They were back inside the station now. Lani had arrived with lights and sirens blaring, which meant the entire town knew something had happened. They'd probably think someone had been stopped for speeding or drunk driving—André hoped so anyway.

"At least let me clean it for you. I think you might need a couple of stitches."

"Graduated from medical school, did you? Or was it the multiple seasons of *Grey's Anatomy?*"

Lani's eyes narrowed and the flare of her nostrils told André he was being an ass. He opened his mouth to apologize when the door burst open, slamming backward into the wall. They both froze, staring at the apparition in front of them. It wasn't Lionel Trent, that was immediately clear.

The hulking figure testing the confines of his black leather jacket and wearing a fierce scowl on his face was Dante Casto-er, Brown. André would recognize him anywhere.

"Police business," Lani said, sharply turning on the intruder, her hand on the service weapon against her hip.

"Gunfire came from this direction. Then sirens." Dante's eyes were wild. His gaze landed on André, and he blanched.

"André," Dante breathed out his name in a way André had never heard before. "What happened?"

"Excuse me," Lani interjected, acid dripped from her tone, but she released her weapon, realizing Dante wasn't a threat. At least, not to anyone in the building. "An expert on ammunition and firearms, are you?"

"Lani," André said—although he appreciated her guard-dog demeanor.

"What?" she snapped, glancing at him.

"This is... a friend of mine, Dante Brown." Brown didn't sound right on his tongue at all. Castone was the name Dante should be using. "He's—he was a cop. I know him." A cop of sorts, but it was too complicated to get into.

"Okay. *Great.* You were a cop. My apologies."

She didn't sound apologetic, but that was Lani. And André had to admit, a person could go either way with Dante—cop or perp.

His laser-blue gaze homing in on André's cheek, Dante took two steps across the lobby to crouch down in front of him.

"What the fuck happened?" Dante whispered, lifting a hand to run a finger down André's wounded face. Was Dante trembling? His voice shaking? No, that couldn't be right. "I—"

"Some asshole took a shot at him, obviously," Lani interrupted.

"Two shots," Dante corrected. "Two fucking bullets aimed right at you."

André nodded. "Two. But, as you can see, they both missed."

"He won't go to the hospital."

Dante managed a passing smile. "Of course, he fucking won't. But." He peered closer. André could smell his aftershave and a hint of sweat, and his cock twitched. "I think a butterfly Band-Aid will do the job. If not, I have some superglue at my place."

"Seriously," Lani demanded, her hands on her hips now. "Who the hell are you, bursting in here like that?"

"Like I said, he's a—"

Dante cut him off. "I'm more than a friend, but André hasn't figured it out yet." He shrugged and looked up at Lani. "To be fair, it took him disappearing on me for me to figure it out. But I'm not doing a vanishing act this time, so maybe he'll finally get a damn clue."

Lani's gaze darted between the two of them. André hoped she knew what Dante was talking about because it was beyond his capability at this point. She seemed to come to the conclusion that Dante at least wasn't an immediate threat.

"Huh. Well, maybe you can talk some sense into him," she muttered.

"I doubt it," Dante said dryly.

"Dante, this is my star deputy, Lani Cooper."

"Cooper, as in Cooper Springs?" Dante asked.

Lani shot a long-suffering gaze upward at the cracked and water-stained plaster ceiling before answering.

"Yep, good old great-great-grandpa. But enough about me. What are we doing about somebody taking shots at the chief?"

Dante rose to his feet, and as he did so, the door opened again. This time it was Deputy Trent.

"What? What'd I miss?" Trent asked as he took in Lani, Dante, and then André. His gaze shot back to Dante and filled with something like trepidation.

Dante growled and Lani's fingers curled into fists. André rose from Carol's chair. His face hurt from the cement chip and the rest of his body hurt from throwing himself to the ground. What he needed was a handful of ibuprofen and his bed. The rest they'd figure out in the morning.

"Someone took a shot at me when I was leaving the building," André explained.

"That's not good, Chief. Did you get a look at the guy?" Lionel looked back and forth between André and Lani and appeared to be shocked. André doubted the man was that good of an actor. Would he try and take André out over being required to attend a seminar? That seemed far-fetched.

"Now that you're here, I'm going to see if the shooter left anything behind," Lani informed them.

The evidence collection class was probably going to be easy for her, André thought.

"Don't go alone. Dante, do you mind?"

He was out of his ever-loving mind asking Dante to help.

"Sure," Dante agreed easily, "but when we get back, I'm taking you home."

That was fine with André. Plus, having them outside would give him a chance to talk to Deputy Lionel Trent. Alone.

TEN

Dante

André would fucking argue with him, that was guaranteed. But no fucking way was a man who'd just been shot at going home to an empty and fucking unsecured house. For fuck's sake, it had taken Dante about thirty seconds to break in and leave the groceries.

"My turn was just back there. Sorry, I should have said." André's voice was rough and thin. The adrenaline must be wearing off.

"I know where I'm going. Thanks though."

After heading east a few more blocks, Dante took a left down the street that ran behind Cooper Mansion, then a right. Thirty seconds later, he pulled in front of his place.

Luckily, Dani was with Romy at Wanda Stone's house, working on a school project. Otherwise, he never would have been wandering around downtown Cooper Springs, trying to drum up the courage to track down André and tell him the truth about why he and Dani were in town. As it was, he'd lost his mind and admitted to having feelings for André in front of his deputy. At least it had been Lani and not the yahoo who'd shown up later.

Just another day in the life of Dante Castone.

"Where are we?" André asked, looking around.

"My place," Dante said shortly.

"Huh. I tried looking up your address, but you aren't listed."

That admission pleased Dante. But on the other hand, maybe he'd been trying to find Dante to tell him never to *drop in* again.

"Nope, we're not. If you come inside and let me fix your face and don't argue, I'll tell you why."

André didn't argue. Instead, he opened the car door and climbed out to follow Dante into the house. Dante didn't think they'd had a tail, but he opened the door as quickly as he could and ushered André inside. From Luna's crate, he heard the dog banging around, ready to be released.

"Come into the kitchen. I need to let the dog out," Dante said as he turned on the lights and opened the crate door.

"Nice place," André said as he *didn't* head to the kitchen like Dante wanted him to. Instead, he took in the crappy sofa and beat-to-crap 1990s TV armoire—was that a thing? Whatever it was, it was hideous. Nothing in the house was stuff Dante would pick out. Sure, his choice of decor tended toward man cave, but black went with everything, right?

"It's not, but you get an A for effort."

That earned him a slight smile. "I hadn't realized that there were still houses with faux wood paneling."

"And matching mustard yellow appliances, not to brag or anything."

The crate door swung open, and Luna bolted out of the crate. She considered sniffing up André but made a beeline for the front door instead. Dante snapped the leash that hung by the door onto her collar.

"I think the color is called Harvest Gold," André corrected as Dante and Luna headed outside, "and my grandmother had a set."

"That you even know that—" Dante shook his head as he and Luna went out the door.

Once Luna had done her business, Dante had no trouble getting her back inside. Usually, she poked her nose around everywhere but tonight, apparently, she wanted to meet André rather than chase every scent she could find.

"Incoming," Dante warned as they came back inside and he unclipped her leash. "I'll be right back, grabbing the first aid."

Was he dragging his feet? Yes, he absolutely was. He didn't want André's sympathy over Simone's death. Snatching the red first aid box out from under the sink, he strode back to the living room. It was conversation time, and he wasn't going to chicken out. After what he'd admitted at the station, saying the rest couldn't be that difficult.

Could it? *Fuck.*

André had risked sitting on the couch and Luna was wiggling all over, demanding pets and trying to climb into his lap even though she knew better. She was not a lap-sized dog.

"Get down," Dante ordered.

Giving him a look that translated to *why are you so mean*, Luna plopped down on her haunches against the couch with her head under André's hand.

"What did you and that Trent character talk about while Cooper and I were outside?" Dante asked. So maybe he wasn't as ready to talk as he'd pretended.

When he and Lani Cooper had returned from not finding anything in or around the parking lot, Deputy Trent had looked like he'd swallowed a lemon. André had looked—aside from like shit because of being shot at—like a man who'd made his point.

Waiting for André's reply, Dante opened the case and plucked out some antiseptic wipes and a butterfly bandage. When André didn't immediately respond, Dante glanced up at him. He was watching Dante with a bemused expression on his face.

"What?" Dante asked as he ripped open the wipe and reached up to start cleaning up the cut on André's cheek.

"What is happening right now? What did you mean back there?"

By *back there*, Dante was going to assume André meant at the station when he'd been so scared and fucking pissed off that he'd blurted out that André was more than a friend to him. In front of one of his deputies. Hopefully, André was out, and Dante hadn't just fucked up everything. What the fuck had he been thinking? He hadn't been using his brain at all. He'd acted on instinct, scared that he'd lost another person who he—liked a lot.

A person he thought could easily be more, who could be a partner. A lover.

"I meant exactly what I said. You're more than a friend to me."

Tossing the used wipe aside, he opened the Band-Aid and gently pressed it over the wound.

"There," he said, leaning away from André so he could see his handiwork. "I don't think you need stitches, but maybe try not to get shot at again."

"I'll do my best," André said, his gaze intent. "You didn't really answer my question."

The hint of a rumble at the end of his sentence had Dante's thoughts heading in another direction. South. Something must have shown in his expression. Lust probably. André always did it for him.

"No," André growled, shooting a glare at Dante's crotch. "I want to know what you meant by not just friends."

With a sigh and a few snaps and pops—he wasn't getting any younger—Dante rose to his feet so he could sit next to André on the couch but a respectable distance apart. He wasn't going to jump him. Not yet anyway.

André twisted to face him, eyebrows raised and one knee

pulled up onto the couch. His fingers still moved restlessly across Luna's head.

"Last time we saw each other in Portland, I was already thinking about getting out. About refusing more undercover assignments, maybe quitting the agency. But I had to finish the one I was on and when I came back, you were gone. I should've come clean with you before, but it seemed like it was never the right time. Or enough time."

Or he'd just been a coward.

There wasn't ever enough time, was there? An image of his sister's smiling face rolled into his head. They'd been very close and now she was gone forever. Dante had lost the chance to tell her how great he thought she was. What an incredible lawyer, mother, and person she was. How without her, he wouldn't be the person he was today.

He didn't want that to happen with André. Maybe they didn't know everything about each other, but he knew André would keep him on his toes, challenge him. And, dammit, that's what he wanted. He suspected André wanted that too.

The man of the hour nudged his knee. "Keep talking."

Dante gathered his thoughts. "Fast forward, I didn't quit. There didn't seem to be a reason to after you disappeared. But believe me when I say I'd been thinking about seeing if you maybe wanted more. More than quickies on our free weekends."

It wasn't André's fault that Dante's job had made it impossible for him to have a real relationship. When he'd taken on the job, he'd only had Simone, with Daniella on the way. Simone had been all for Dante's career, proud that he played an important part in taking down human trafficking organizations, drug dealers, and other scum. "Then in August, my sister was murdered. And everything changed."

"Your sister."

"Yes."

"I'm sorry."

His tone encompassed the things that there were no words for. The pain and grief of losing a loved one forever.

"I am too. Anyway. Dani witnessed it and"—he raised a hand, palm out—"yes, we were offered WITSEC, but we decided against it. The choice was made, and neither Dani nor I are changing our minds. Case closed."

André looked away from him to stare at nothing, nostrils flared. He was clearly working hard not to fly off the handle. Marshals felt strongly about WITSEC, even retired ones.

"We'll circle back to that issue later." André turned back to him. "How did you end up in Cooper Springs? I have a hard time believing it was an accident."

"Definitely one hundred percent on purpose," Dante admitted. "It wasn't hard to figure out where you'd moved to. Once I knew my UC life was done and I had Dani to keep safe, I had the wild thought that, now that I wasn't undercover, we might as well move to Cooper Springs. The guys who killed Simone would never think of looking here, and we're using Brown, just in case. But I also thought, why not come here and make a case for myself? Damn." He paused. "I didn't out you, did I?"

"No, you didn't. Not that I shout my sexuality everywhere. But seriously. One." André raised his thumb. "You've been here since at least September—that's three plus months. Two." He lifted his index finger. "*Making your case* is not showing up at my house and fucking me into the mattress." Now he pointed his finger gun at Dante.

Wincing at the truth of André's words, Dante crossed his arms over his chest. André wasn't going to make this easy. But did he want easy?

No. He wanted André Dear, who was not at all simple. Or easy.

"That was a mistake. Not the sex part," he rushed, "but the

just sex part. Seeing you again close up and personal, I kind of lost my head. And then—well, it's different for me now, isn't it? I have Dani to think of. I can't just drop in unannounced and strip you naked whenever I want—which is *always*, just so you know —and—"

He had to push aside a memory of him and André naked together in bed or he was never going to finish.

"Know that I always want to. Being a full-time uncle is harder than I ever expected. And I worry about Dani. Hatch, my old handler, called last week to tell me that there's been rumors. They're pretty sure a criminal already in the Big House is up to something. Maybe."

"What kind of something?" André's concern overtook his previous irritation.

"Maybe Dani heard her mom talking on the phone and didn't know that she heard something important? I honestly don't know. She was careful, a professional. Damn good at her job—she wouldn't talk to her kid about any of her cases, but especially not about fucks like this shit."

Simone's only mistake was opening the door that night.

"Huh. Your sister was in law enforcement too?"

"Sort of."

They'd strayed from André's original question, but after a brief moment of looking thoughtful, André brought them full circle.

"So, you came here to hide, a DIY protection program. You have to know that, as an ex-marshal, I absolutely hate that decision. But" —he shook his head, appearing bemused once again— "you really came here because *I'm* here? Were you planning on luring me out to a balcony and declaring yourself?"

Dante scowled at André. Now André looked amused. Yes, he felt fucking defensive.

"Maybe? Maybe I was. But then we got here, and things have

been fucking hard. And maybe I don't know what love is anyway." There, he'd used The Word. "But I do know that I enjoy being with you and I haven't been with anyone since you left Portland."

"Really?"

"Christ." His patience was starting to fray. "André, I haven't been with anyone else since the first night we went home together. That's closing in on two years."

They were both quiet for a moment, thinking about that first night. Dante had to shift in his seat again. That had been fucking intense.

"So... what you're saying is that you've been in a relationship with me, and I didn't know it? Am I that oblivious?"

Dante relaxed his shoulders. André wasn't denying that there had been something more than just sex between them. "Maybe we're both a little slow on the uptake?"

André eyed him, nodding slowly.

"What if you moved here and I was with someone else?"

That was something Dante hadn't let himself think about. Also, he was a grown-ass man, and look, here he was using his words.

"But you aren't, are you?" Dante was ninety-nine percent sure André wasn't dating anyone. He wouldn't have let Dante in the house that night if he was involved with another man.

André's eyebrows drew together. "No, but that's not the point."

It was totally Dante's point.

"Have you been with anyone else?"

After a slight pause, Dante saw André's expression change as he realized that there'd been no one but Dante. At least, he hoped that's what it was because otherwise the smug feeling in his chest was over nothing.

"No. No, I haven't."

Dante made no attempt to hide his satisfied grin. However, a growling sound that was not Luna emanated from André's stomach and had him frowning again.

"Sorry. I guess I'm hungry."

Dante would feed him in a minute. He couldn't stop now, even if he could almost hear his Italian grandmother berating him for not immediately rushing into the kitchen.

"Do you want to be with someone else?" He needed to make absolutely certain he wasn't making an ass of himself. Or maybe declaring sincere and deep feelings for someone made everyone feel like they'd just jumped out of a perfectly good airplane.

"Obviously not," André snapped back. "I've been here almost a year, I am definitely still single, and no, I don't want to be with someone else." Nodding, he nibbled thoughtfully at his lower lip. "So, this grocery buying and breaking into my house, bringing me dinner. This is you... flirting?"

"I'd say more like wooing."

"Wooing," André repeated with a snort and a raised eyebrow.

"Wooing," Dante confirmed. "And absolutely not creepy at all."

"But you're still basically in hiding. Dani saw something, maybe can ID the killer?"

"Dani witnessed the murder, yeah. She was at the top of the stairs."

He hated talking about Simone's death. He hated his brain for being too good at imagining the scene in vivid color and slow motion.

"And said scumbag knows this?"

"Presumably. The hired gunmen were found dead in a field outside of Salem. I was told it wasn't pretty."

"And they know Dani was there." André didn't sound like the idea surprised him.

They was Aldo Campos, but André didn't need to know that. The fewer who knew, the better.

"You know as well as I do that LEOs talk. I was on assignment in eastern Oregon and didn't get to her until she'd been transported to the downtown station. Hatch got to her as fast as he could, but someone other than the actual killers knows Dani was there."

"If the shooters are dead, why is she still in danger?"

"They were only able to ID one of them. The second could be gunman number two or could just be someone with the worst luck."

"Fuck."

"Fuck," Dante agreed. "Let's talk about something else. Who do you think took a shot at you?"

André shifted toward him, earning a pout and a flop onto the rug from Luna. "How about we keep talking about this wooing?"

"How about we forget I used that word?" Dante's cheeks felt hot.

Now André smiled—and then winced because he'd obviously forgotten about the injury to his cheek. "Mm, nope."

Dante hung his head in mock despair. "Damn."

"You really moved here for me?"

He appeared to be genuinely shocked. His reaction made Dante wonder about André's past.

"Well, I suppose I moved here for *me*. Dani too. But it was still a very selfish act. Like I said, I'd wondered about *us* before you left town, about seeing if we could make it work. If you'd be interested in more than me stopping by between assignments or on my weekends off and taking you away from your evening tea and reading. It just took me a bit to realize that's what it was."

André's lips parted, maybe to deny his reading habit, but Dante never found out. A pounding in the front door had both of them startling.

"Dante Castone, open up," a deep, muffled voice demanded. A voice Dante was pretty sure he recognized, but he was feeling mighty paranoid these days.

He glanced at André, who frowned and shook his head.

"Get into the kitchen," he demanded.

"Fuck that. You want us to start something, it's not beginning with me hiding in the kitchen."

"Always you have to argue."

"You love it."

"I do," Dante admitted.

ELEVEN

André

André was only minimally relieved to learn that the uninvited guest turned out to be someone from the life Dante had recently left behind. A coworker, apparently. Did the guy have to choose this exact minute to interrupt their conversation? There were things André needed to say and questions he still needed to ask.

After the day he'd had, he thought he might have enjoyed a messy takedown as long as he emerged unscathed. Being closer to fifty than forty had some pros—he was still alive and kicking, after all—but age also had its downsides. Like the fact that his right shoulder throbbed along with his face. And it would be a few days before he shook off the aches and pains, not just by tomorrow morning.

"Fuck you, Morrison," Dante rumbled at the giant waiting on his tiny porch. "Did you have to knock on my door like some kind of enforcer?"

André didn't bother to hide his smirk at the complaint. Dante didn't really have an argument seeing as how he also liked to use a heavy fist when he pounded on people's doors.

Luna hadn't barked, which surprised André. Instead, she lurked in the shadows of the front room with her tail slightly lowered. The dog eyed the open door, watching Morrison as if to determine whether he was friend or foe. She must have decided he was no immediate threat because she shook out her entire body before padding over to lean against André's thigh.

"Eh." The man spread his hands apart, palms outward, in a gesture of peace. "I don't get out much these days. Hatch keeps me on a short leash."

Morrison filled the entire doorframe. He was a giant of a man with thick, curly hair that was absolutely not regulation. Undercover for certain, or maybe he just did what he wanted.

"I can't imagine why," Dante scoffed, backing away from the porch and motioning Morrison inside.

André's stomach chose that moment to growl again, even louder than a few moments ago. Both men turned to look at him. Morrison paused with one foot raised over the threshold, obviously impressed by the volume, and Dante's scowl deepened. With an exasperated huff, he pulled Morrison inside and slammed and locked the door shut behind him.

"I suppose I'm feeding you too?" he asked his visitor.

Morrison plastered a ridiculous smile on his face and batted his eyes at Dante. André wondered how good of friends they were. Had they worked closely together or were they just in the same office?

"I could eat," Morrison agreed with enthusiasm. "But we need to have a conversation." The big man shot an inquiring glance toward André. "What happened to your face?"

Instinctively, André lifted his hand, touching the bandage stuck to his cheek. He'd managed to forget he'd been shot at for several seconds. It wasn't something he could ignore forever though.

Who the hell had it in for him? Had the shots been meant

only to scare him, or did the shooter have terrible aim? André wasn't sure which answer he preferred.

"Let's talk in the kitchen. First, you can tell me why Hatch didn't warn me you were coming," said Dante.

Morrison shot André a skeptical look. "André's good," Dante added. "I vouch for him. To answer your question, somebody took a shot at him earlier tonight."

Without waiting for Morrison to voice an objection, Dante turned and headed into the kitchen. Glancing at André again, Morrison shrugged and followed Dante. André paused and allowed himself to briefly contemplate the fact that Dante would vouch for him before joining them.

Huh.

"André, this is Ivan Morrison," Dante said when André stepped into the kitchen. "Morrison, this is André Dear, Cooper Spring's chief of police."

Morrison's dark eyebrows rose in surprise—or appreciation? André wasn't sure which—and stuck his hand out toward André.

"It's a pleasure," Ivan said. "Please, just call me Morrison."

"I'm going to throw some pasta sauce together while you tell me what the fuck brought you here, so get talking." Dante started rummaging through pots and pans and grabbing ingredients out of his refrigerator.

"Ivan Morrison," André repeated slowly before Morrison could speak. He rolled the name around in his head. Morrison's eyes narrowed. "As in Van Morrison, the musician?"

Groaning and shaking his head in disgust, Morrison sucked a long breath in through his nose at André's question. Dante turned away from the cupboard he'd opened, waiting expectantly.

"Years!" he finally exclaimed, throwing his hands up dramatically. "*Years*, it's been since the last time someone figured out that *my own mother* named me after Van Morrison. I thought I was finally safe."

Dante snickered and started filling a large pot with water before setting it on the stove.

"It's not the worst superstar to be named after," André pointed out.

"Meh." Morrison's bushy eyebrows drew together. "I feel like I'm more Chris Hemsworth than moldy old Irish folk singer. I mean, look at me." He swept his hands down the bulk of himself.

André had to admit he had a point. Dante's biceps looked like twigs compared to what André suspected was hidden underneath Morrison's jacket.

"Especially since you can't sing," Dante said. "Ivan's been banned from karaoke night. I think the exact words were, *never again.*"

"Did I tell you to fuck off already? I haven't? Fuck off. Do you want to know why Hatch sent me here or not? And don't call me Ivan."

Suppressing a grin, André took a seat at the round kitchen table, noting that the kitchen appliances were indeed Harvest Gold. Grumbling about his mother and traitorous friends, Morrison peeled off his black leather motorcycle jacket—confirming André's suspicion about the size of his arms—and hung it over the back of a well-used chair. Before setting his full weight on it, he gingerly tested the piece of furniture to see if it would hold. When he didn't end up sitting in a pile of toothpicks, he shot a triumphant grin at André.

"So, Hatch?" Dante said while he peeled and minced onions.

"Right. It's not good. He suspects the office is compromised. Information that shouldn't be is getting out to people who have no business learning it. He didn't even want to email you. In person only."

"Example," Dante demanded as he tossed a handful of the chopped onions into a saucepan with a dollop of olive oil. The pungent scent of the cooking vegetables had André's insides complaining again.

"Can you tell your damn stomach I'm cooking as fast as I can?"

A second rumble came from Morrison's direction.

"Do neither of you eat?" he asked.

This was a question André wasn't bothering to answer and Morrison just shot him a toothy grin.

"The job you were on this summer," Morrison said, returning to the matter at hand. "Someone got wind of the operation. We were able to sweep up a few guys, but no one of any importance. Not one of them had any useful information about where their funding was coming from or where the inventory went once it was out of their hands. Human trafficking scum-fuckers of the earth."

There was no arguing with that assessment.

"That's damn unfortunate." Dante added garlic to the pan, its spicy aroma instantly filling the kitchen. "Years of fucking work went into that op. Does Hatch have any ideas who the leak is?"

Regardless of his hunger pangs and Dante and Morrison's conversation, André started thinking about who could have taken a shot at him. For the life of him, he couldn't come up with an immediate suspect. It wasn't as if Cooper Springs was Mayberry, and he very much wasn't Andy Taylor—the fictional sheriff had been much more patient than André. But André didn't think he'd made any enemies in town. Not anyone who hated him enough to try and kill him anyway.

"André, can you hand me a sleeve of pasta?" Dante asked. "There should be some in the cabinet behind me. I can't stop stirring or the garlic will burn."

"Sure." André rose to his feet, crossing over to the cabinet Dante had indicated.

As he leaned down to open the cabinet, Morrison said, "Yeah, so we think someone in the office has been compromised, but they're good at hiding their tracks."

André took in the contents of the cupboard. There was no

pasta in boxes or in plastic sleeves. He did, however, see a Glock. Not his—his was secured in a concealed Kydex holster.

"Dante, there's nothing in here but your spare weapon."

André bent down to look more carefully, in case he was just not seeing the spaghetti.

Behind him, Morrison laughed. "That's Dante, can't use a gun safe. Gotta be original."

"Look, Dani's not gonna touch it," Dante protested, his voice rising, "and I'm not gonna be caught with my pants down and my spare weapon locked where I can't fucking get to it."

"You gotta keep your pants on in the kitchen. I got a grease burn once on my ass and damn did it hurt."

There was a long silence while André at least processed what Morrison had just said.

"TMI, big guy," Dante said. "And please don't derail the conversation with your ass. André, maybe check the next one over. I'm still getting used to this kitchen."

André opened the next cupboard and found the pasta stash. Selecting a bag of spaghetti, he set it on the counter next to Dante.

"Damn, I'm hungrier than I realized," Morrison said. "Thanks for feeding me."

"I'm sure I'll regret it. Now, tell me everything you can from the beginning."

André leaned his butt back against the counter, watching Dante cook while Morrison rehashed the information he'd been sent to Cooper Springs to share. The operation Dante had been a part of wasn't the only one that had been compromised. The agency had been forced to abandon a second op after a key inside man had been found in several pieces shoved inside a garbage bin in downtown Portland.

"Damn, Hatch and the uppers spent at least two years getting someone inside that organization," Dante interjected.

The names Morrison mentioned weren't familiar to André. The agencies often worked together, but his last months with the Marshals Service had primarily been working protection assignments. The only thing André had left from his old life was to testify in the State vs. Campos trial, and that wasn't set to begin for another six months after the prosecutor's death. Jensen would have contacted him if he needed to be concerned about anything.

"Hatch thinks whoever it is, they're trying to find you," Morrison added.

That had André paying attention again. Dante was a pain in his ass, but he was André's pain in the ass—something he was still working on processing. But he and Dani were also residents of Cooper Springs and therefore under André's protection.

"Maybe it's a good thing you didn't go into the system after all," Morrison finished. "Maybe you would've been found by now."

"The marshals' system is tight," André protested. WITSEC was need-to-know only and sometimes not even that. Once, he'd been assigned to a mother who was testifying against some Very Bad People, one of whom was her ex-husband, and André alone had known where she and her son were hiding. "Could it be this Hatch guy you keep mentioning? It wouldn't be the first time someone higher up has been compromised."

Both men turned to look at him. Morrison looked thoughtful, and Dante shook his head.

"Anything is possible. But, except for sending Morrison, Hatch hasn't done anything to make me think he's on the take."

"No system—not even the U.S. Marshals'—is safe from the inside," Morrison said blandly. "Whoever is behind this shit has some computer chops."

André knew he was right, but he didn't have to like it.

"I guess we can rule you out, Morrison," Dante said dryly as he began to scoop pasta and sauce onto dinner plates. "Here," he said to André, pointing at a plate with more food than André had eaten in several days piled on it, "take that one."

Without arguing, André took the plate back to the table and sat down, sensing that Dante would force-feed him if he complained. Morrison side-eyed his meal.

"You can have half of mine," he whispered.

Morrison gave him a thumbs-up as he accepted a dish from Dante.

Grabbing the third serving, Dante sat down next to André and began to swirl noodles onto his fork.

"So, you've delivered Hatch's message. What am I supposed to do about it?"

"You and Daniella could still go into WITSEC," André pointed out. Luckily, Dante had just shoved a huge bite into his mouth so he couldn't reply.

"Nah, I don't think they should," said Morrison, "Hatch is on edge. He wants you to be vigilant."

"That's what he said when we spoke on the phone. As if I'm ever *not* vigilant."

"He also instructed me to stick around town for a bit, keep my eye on you." Morrison crossed his massive arms over his chest as if daring Dante to argue.

"I can't believe you're giving me crap about protection when you won't accept it for you and your niece," André complained. "Kettle meet pot."

"Shit, Dani." Shooting to his feet, Dante glanced at his watch and shoved another forkful of pasta into his mouth. "I need to pick her up. You." He pointed at André. "Do not leave. You." Now his finger was directed at Morrison. "Stay here and keep an eye on him. Do. Not. Let. Him. Leave."

Then Dante was gone. It was very easy for André to imagine a dust devil swirling in his wake. In the ensuing silence, André and Morrison eyed each other.

"Am I gonna have to tie you up?" Morrison asked.

Was that an amused gleam in Morrison's eyes?

"Nope," André said, quickly forking more spaghetti into his mouth.

He'd wait until Dante returned and then he'd leave.

"This is not what I meant when I said I was going home," André said as he slid his key into the deadbolt. He was comfortably full from dinner and Morrison had finished off what André hadn't been able to eat.

"I have to say," Morrison rumbled, "that I enjoyed being on the sidelines for that one. How long have you and our Dante been together?"

The door eased open, and André started inside.

"Dante and I are—" André cut himself off, trying to figure out the words to explain it to his unwelcome bodyguard. "It's complicated."

André always wanted Dante; he wasn't going to deny that part of their relationship. If Morrison hadn't interrupted them, maybe they would have had a chance to talk things out more. Was Dante planning on staying in Cooper Springs? Did he see them sharing a home? Did he see André as a partner?

"Why do people always make easy things difficult for themselves? If you click, you click. It's that simple."

"So you say," André responded, twisting the door knob.

"Wait." Morrison lay a meaty hand on his shoulder. "Let me make sure it's clear."

There was no point arguing with him. André waited impatiently in the living room while Morrison checked all the rooms in the house and his backyard as well.

"Nice house you've got. That backyard is damn big. You should put in a patio and one of those propane heaters."

"Thanks for the tip," André managed.

His cheek hurt from the cement chip. His jaw ached from clenching it. And instead of having Dante in his bed and the possibility of all sorts of *relaxation* going on, he was saddled with an unnecessary bodyguard whose brain-to-mouth filter needed some adjustments.

TWELVE

Dante

"Be extra careful today and for the next few days. I know it's hard but try not to let your guard down. If you see anything out of the ordinary or get a funny feeling, call me and I will come to you right away."

Dani turned her head and just stared at him for a moment.

"Has something happened?" she finally asked.

Dante had decided months ago not to sugarcoat anything about their situation. He didn't want to scare her, but it wasn't fair to be left in the dark. Ignorance was not bliss.

"My old boss is concerned—that's why Morrison showed up last night. I just want you to be careful."

"Okay, Zio."

"Morrison might be the one picking you up today."

"Okay, Zio. I like him."

"He's the only one I trust."

"What about Chief Dear?"

Dante sighed. "Fine, yes, I trust him too. But I doubt he'll be the one picking you up. It'll be me or Morrison. If anyone else—

and I mean *anyone*—approaches you, run back inside to the office and wait for one of us."

When she didn't immediately get out of the car, Dante raised his eyebrows and poked her in the ribs.

"Get going."

"I like Chief Dear too, Zio. He has kind eyes."

Now her expression had a hint of mischief to it. Was she trying to trick him into admitting he had feelings for André?

He affixed a firm and hopefully unrevealing expression on his face. "He does. Now get going," he repeated.

With a grin that told him he hadn't fooled her one bit, Dani got out and headed toward the school building.

Once the high school doors closed behind her, Dante pointed his car toward downtown Cooper Springs and the police station. André had not replied to his texts this morning, but Morrison had.

"May I help you?"

The older woman from his visit in December was perched on a chair behind the desk in the station's lobby. A placard sitting front and center read: *Carol Page.*

"I need to talk to André. To Chief Dear."

This woman had not been here yesterday when Dante had come barreling in to check on André. But it was clear from her demeanor that this was her domain and he had to pass inspection to get any further.

"I remember you from December. And heard a bit from Chief Dear after that?" The woman's smile was backed with steel. "Chief Dear has a press conference in less than an hour and asked not to be disturbed."

"Sorry about that, truly. But if you could let him know that Dante Brown is here? Also, has a very large man been hanging around?"

A smile bloomed on Carol's face. "Ivan? He's in the break-room down that hallway." She gestured behind her and to the right. "I'm afraid the chief's office wasn't comfortable for the both of them. Ivan!" she called out. "There's someone here asking about you." Turning her attention back to Dante, she said, "I'll inform the chief you're here."

The floor vibrated, announcing the arrival of Morrison. He'd allowed Carol to use his first name? What other superpowers did the woman have? Dante wasn't sure he wanted to know. And he now suspected he hadn't fooled her as much as he'd thought when he got André's number from her.

"Hey, Cast—Brown. What kind of name is Brown anyway? A first grader could do better." He eyed Carol. "Forget I said anything."

She mimed zipping her lips. "Consider it forgotten."

"Come on back," Morrison invited. "I think we can both fit in the breakroom."

The breakroom wasn't so much a room as a niche between the lobby and a door labeled *Armory*, but there was a coffee maker, two plastic chairs, and a small table that looked like it had been rescued from a burning building.

"Coffee?" Morrison asked.

Dante eyed the machine with a great deal of skepticism. He came from a long line of coffee snobs.

"It's drinkable, I promise." He leaned toward Dante and continued in—for Morrison—a hushed tone, "Have a cup so you don't hurt Carol's feelings."

Wondering what the fuck was happening in his world that a senior citizen had charmed Ivan Morrison, Dante grabbed a cracked but clean-looking mug and filled it with coffee. Then he proceeded to add three creamers and three sugars. Morrison watched with disgust.

"How do you drink it like that?" He shuddered.

Dante ignored him and took a sip of the hot brew. The cream and sugar masked the bitter flavor.

"What's the news conference this morning about?"

Was André going public about being shot at yesterday? That would surprise Dante. Taking a second sip of the doctored coffee, Dante waited for Morrison's reply.

The big man sat down first, one elbow on the scarred table. Rolling his eyes, Dante sat down as well.

"I assume you know about the remains that have been discovered over the past few months? Today was the first I'd heard about them."

Dante nodded.

"Right. Well, it's about them. André told me the mayor arranged for a forensic anthropologist to come in and help excavate and identify them. Turns out he's her son—not André, the anthropologist guy. Anyway"—Morrison waved a large hand, almost knocking over his own mug—"he arrived about an hour ago, and he and André are holed up nailing down what to say and how to spin it."

"Huh."

It had been a long night for Dante, with little sleep. His skin felt twitchy and too fucking tight. He needed to lay eyes on André, to prove to himself firsthand that the man was still in one piece. Last night he'd forced himself to focus on Daniella instead of texting André, but it had been close to impossible. Having Morrison around to keep an eye on André made Dante feel slightly better—even if that's not what Hatch had intended by sending him to Cooper Springs. The issue was that Dante wanted to keep watch over André himself, forever and always.

Fuck. Fucking hell.

Dante rubbed his chest, directly over his pounding heart. He could almost hear Simone in his head, laughing her ass off at his predicament. She'd teased him forever about being a player, using his job as an excuse not to settle down.

"When you fall, *fratello mio*, it's going to be fast and hard and forever. I kind of feel bad for whoever it turns out to be. The man will need the patience of a saint." She'd paused, watching him closely over her glass of merlot. "No, actually, I feel sorry for you. You aren't going to have the first clue what to do. I'll give you a hint—try not to be a caveman."

Morrison cleared his throat and Dante looked across the table. He must have been quiet for too long.

"What?"

"How do you want to play this? The news conference is in twenty minutes."

As much as Dante wanted to protect André himself with his own body, to stand menacingly at his side, he did not want to end up with his face on national TV. That was not lying low. If that happened, he would deserve the scorn André would shower on him.

"You stay here with André." *Guard him as if your life depends on his survival* was implied. He drained the last of his coffee in one sugary rush. Rising from the table, he rinsed the cup out in the tiny sink and set it on the counter. "I'm going to check in with him and then I have a few things I want to follow up on today."

"Anything you're willing to fill me in on?"

Dante shook his head. "Nope. Not yet, anyway."

Abandoning Morrison in the tiny room, Dante went back out and around the front desk, then down the corridor where he assumed André's office was. The first door he opened, however, was not what he was looking for. The space wasn't much bigger than the breakroom, but instead of a table and chairs, there were sets of shelves and each one was packed tight with cardboard boxes. The boxes had dates marked on them with permanent marker or ballpoint and were labeled *Evidence*. There was no room for more.

"Jesus Christ."

He shut the door and continued to the last door along the

hall. Just past it was the exit to the parking lot. Without knocking —that way, André couldn't say no—he twisted the handle and pushed it open, nearly banging the door into the back of the occupied visitor's chair.

"Oh, hello, Dante." André's lips did something complicated, hinting he was amused by Dante's entrance, and he glanced at his watch. "I'm impressed it took you this long to get here. Ethan Moore, this is... an associate of mine, Dante Brown." Dante felt his hackles rise at André's use of the word associate. "Dante, this is Ethan Moore. He's going to be leading the team recovering and identifying the remains."

Ethan Moore looked to be in his forties. His dark hair was just beginning to go gray at his temples and he had the skin tone of someone who spent time in the sun. Crow's feet had formed at the corners of his eyes.

"It's a pleasure," Ethan said, standing up and offering Dante his hand. "Well," he amended, "the reason I'm here isn't a pleasure, but closure is important, and that's why I do this."

Against his better judgment, Dante immediately liked Moore.

During his career in law enforcement, Dante had found that the forensic community could be roughly divided into two categories. The first were those who created a thick wall between themselves and the work they did. They were not compassionate; for whatever reason, they couldn't afford to be. Remains were a job to them, and one they wanted to get through as quickly as possible.

Then there were those who treated every scrap of fabric, every bone shard, and every possible piece of evidence with respect and kindness. Kindness that very possibly the person had never received while they were living. These forensic scientists didn't refer to remains as victims if they knew the name that belonged to them.

Dante suspected Ethan was one of the latter. He also suspected being compassionate took a great deal out of them.

Looking at him more closely, Dante revised his age guess down a few years—late thirties, at most.

Dante shook the proffered hand. "It's a pleasure to meet you as well." See, he could be pleasant.

"I'll see you on the front steps in a few minutes," Ethan said to André before he departed.

Dante was too twitchy to sit, and André would be leaving soon anyway. Plus, he had a proposition for the chief.

"You need help," he started.

"Nothing new there. No time to see a therapist."

"Ha ha. What I mean is, you've got too many pots and not enough cooks. Let me take some of it off your hands."

"I've got Lani looking into some angles."

"Obtuse or oblique? Because from where I'm standing, it looks like you are two people trying to hold back a shitstorm. Bring me on as an advisor or something and give me access to the department records."

He held up his hand and ticked off the list he'd made in his head. "You've got a missing girl, Blair Cruz. You've got a dead local woman, Lizzy Harlow. And now you've got more than one set of remains from up on that mountain. Oh, and somebody shooting at you."

"Thanks for telling me what I already knew," André snapped.

He'd pissed him off. Well, nothing new about that. Dante enjoyed André pissed off and ready to take names.

Now was not the time.

"What do you know about the chief you took over from?" Dante asked, diverting himself from sexy thoughts. "Did they run a tight ship? Keep good records?"

The heartfelt sigh that escaped André was enough of an answer. Dante was now sure that what he wanted to propose was a good idea. The key would be getting André to go along with it.

"Maybe I can't help directly with the missing teen or the Harlow case, but I can go through old records and look for patterns that may have been missed." Or never looked for in the first place. "I'd like to go over the missing persons reports going back as far as the eighties. If whoever is responsible started young —well, you and I both know it's possible this has been going on for a long time. You don't have the time or the people power. I do." Dante wasn't an investigator per se, but he knew his way around police reports.

André leaned back in his chair to glare at Dante. "Seriously? You're going to try and interfere with an ongoing investigation?"

The glare was a half-hearted effort, not one of André's best.

"That's a damn flimsy argument, *Chief*. You know as well as I do that you don't have enough deputies for this. Are you going to enlist Carol now? Where is that other guy? The one who showed up last night?"

"Carol is retiring," André muttered grimly.

"Ah, that's lovely. So you'll be even more short-staffed than you already are."

Dante moved so he was directly next to the desk and yeah, maybe so he could loom a little. He enjoyed the occasional loom. He watched André, closely spotting when the irritation and frustration began to morph into something else. Something that had Dante's cock reacting—again.

"I'll think about it." André stood from his chair and began to fiddle with the files sitting on his desk. Dante also noticed he still looked tired and like he was nursing a headache, and the damn bandage on his cheek was a reminder he'd nearly been killed. If he'd stepped in a different direction or moved his head, the town would be planning a funeral. André's funeral.

"Morrison's going to stick around during the news conference," Dante informed him.

André looked at him sharply as he edged around the desk. He stopped moving, paperwork in his hands as his lips thinned even further.

"You have it all worked out, do you? You're going to protect me even if I don't need protection? You do realize I've done just fine taking care of myself for nearly fifty years?"

Dante opened his mouth to point out that he wasn't the one who'd been shot at, but André just kept talking.

"Aren't *you* the one hiding out? Don't you have a niece to watch after? Something better to do than show up and stick your nose into *my* business?"

Before Dante realized he was moving, he'd stepped directly into André's space. They were chest to chest now. Dante could feel his heart beating—or maybe it was both their hearts, his and André's together. He wasn't so much *in* André's space as invading him, claiming André for his own.

But it wasn't Dante who acted first. With a groan of frustration and a deep growl, André pushed Dante the last few inches to the wall behind them.

"You drive me fucking crazy."

Dante's shoulders banged against it with a resounding thump, the door vibrating in its frame.

"You love it."

It was André who claimed Dante's lips and mouth. It was André who proceeded to ravage him as if it had been years, not just a few weeks, since they'd last kissed. It was André who gripped the back of Dante's neck and demanded entrance into his mouth.

"Jesus Christ," Dante whimpered, opening up. He was half hard already, his cock reveling in the pressure of André's body against him. He pressed his hips harder back against André. He needed more.

Snaking a hand between them, André cupped and gently squeezed Dante's denim-covered erection.

"Fuck, André," Dante groaned. They were a mere hairsbreadth away from a bad decision.

André's hand fell away. Relinquishing Dante's mouth, he leaned his forehead against Dante's. They were breathing heavily.

And they were both hard, but sex in André's office was definitely some kind of code violation—even Dante knew that. And there was the press conference in—Dante breathed in and glanced at his watch—five minutes.

"You've got people waiting. We'll finish this later. Think about my offer."

THIRTEEN

André

Did it look like he and Dante Castone had been about to rip each other's clothes off and fuck? In his office? And before a major press conference? Could he have acted in a more unprofessional manner? No. The answer was definitely no.

For the third or fourth time, André smoothed his slacks and made certain his shirt was buttoned and tucked in properly. How the hell did Dante manage to get under his skin so quickly?

Dante had left the station by the time André was ready to emerge from the relative safety of his office. He'd needed a minute to calm down, to think about unpleasant things. Things that made his erection subside—like the sad pile of bones that had once been living, breathing humans. That had done the trick.

Now, here he was in the eye of the storm. Three news vans were parked along the sidewalk—it was tempting to threaten them all with tickets for taking up the no-parking zone. But he restrained himself. Might as well try to start on good footing. Thankfully, two representatives from West Coast Forensics had arrived along with Ethan Moore. André would not be doing the press conference alone.

The larger-than-life ex-homicide detective from Seattle wasn't a surprise. Sacha Bolic was. André stared at him. Sacha smirked back.

"Keeping my hand in. Wouldn't want my skills to get rusty."

"I think that's the idea behind retirement," André said dryly.

"Meh, retirement is whatever you want it to be," he replied before stepping back and managing to disappear even though André knew he was right there.

"I'm not normally involved in this crap," Niall Hamarsson said from the side of his mouth as he continued to glare at the reporters and video crew. André needed to up his glare game. Hamarsson had it down to an art. "In this case, Frye seems to think just my presence will keep the yahoos from getting out of control."

André wasn't going to argue. He suspected that Hamarsson was hoping the press might step out of line so he could grab one or two of them by the collar and shake them like bad dogs. There was something ominous about the ex-homicide detective turned WCF cold case investigator. If André had seen him on the street and hadn't already been introduced to him, he would have steered clear of the man.

"We appreciate it."

Squinting across the highway toward the ocean, André could just make out the tiny figures of who he knew to be Martin Purdy and Nick Waugh. They and two contractors were working on the roofs of the cabins that made up Cooper Springs Resort. The sight reminded André that he needed to follow up with Waugh about the soon-to-be-vacant dispatch position and run a background check on him as well. André trusted Carol's recommendation—with reservation—but all the boxes needed to be checked. He didn't want to be saddled with another employee like Deputy Trent.

"Ready?" Hamarsson asked.

The reporters, sensing things were about to begin, surged forward, each trying to be closest to the front.

"As I'll ever be."

Because he was a bastard too, André first read the prepared statement that pretty much said nothing. What was there to say? After rehashing what they already knew, he agreed to answer a few questions and started with the younger male reporter who had been relegated to the back row.

"Yes? You in the back with the black cap."

The reporter appeared to be about twenty-two, young enough to be André's child. He looked around himself as if André might possibly have been talking to another person in a black cap.

"Oh, uh, me?" He cleared his throat and spoke louder. "Do you think there's a serial killer on the loose?"

"Well, that wasn't a complete disaster," André remarked. "Except for the serial killer part." That had basically ended up being the last question as the other newscasters had immediately added their serial killer-related questions, to all of which André responded *no comment*.

Moore, Hamarsson, André, Morrison, and Bolic had taken over the lobby of the station. André had tried to get rid of Morrison, but he just shook his head and claimed the seat behind Carol's desk. Carol was enjoying her lunch break, and the room was hardly big enough for the five of them. Six would have been impossible.

"The serial killer groupies will be next," Hamarsson said morosely. "With luck, most of them will fuck off once they realize there's nowhere in town to stay. But, fair warning, a few will stick around and do their best to make your life miserable."

Sacha nodded from his perch against Carol's desk. Like

André's, the thing dated back to the fifties and could probably hold three of Sacha.

"As long as I don't have any of them following us up to the site," Moore said grimly. He'd leaned one shoulder against the wall, his arms folded across his chest. André had been impressed by his calm demeanor during the press conference. The man had clearly been a part of more than one.

Hamarsson snorted derisively. "You totally will, Ethan. Be prepared."

André wasn't so sure. After he'd hiked up to the site with Martin, Mags, and Critter, he'd concluded that he wasn't in as good of shape as he'd thought. Sitting behind a desk did that to a person.

Note to self: add a fitness regimen to his schedule.

"The last thing I need is someone messing with what's up there," Moore grumbled. "Or getting lost, forcing us to waste resources finding them."

"Unpopular opinion," Sacha rumbled, "but if someone gets lost up there trying to find the site, they get what they deserve."

"With any luck, the weather will keep people away," André added. "Regardless, Critter and Mags have offered to keep an eye on the trailhead. And when they're not available, one of my deputies will be there. It's the best we can do."

"I'll take a shift. It's been a while since I was legally allowed to intimidate anyone," said Sacha.

Ethan nodded and glanced over at Sacha, then at André. "I'm sorry, did you say Critter? Mags?"

"Ah." André smiled, thinking about two of his favorite people in Cooper Springs. "Mike Zweig—aka Critter—and Mags Serle. They're the forest service around these parts."

A well of satisfaction surged in his chest for finding a way to use *these parts* in a sentence. Hamarsson raised one dark eyebrow at him and shook his head.

"How long do you think you need?" André asked Ethan. The

excavation could only take a couple of days, but he knew it might be weeks before they were finished. They still didn't even have an idea of the true size of the scene—all they'd done so far was wrap crime scene tape around what they'd found. Hopefully, evidence hadn't been crushed under hikers' boots or moved far away by forest creatures.

A crease formed between Moore's eyebrows as he pondered André's question. "It's difficult to say since we don't have an idea yet how far the site extends. Could be three days, could be three weeks."

André sucked in a breath; fingers crossed that it didn't take that long.

"Are the feds interested yet?" Hamarsson asked.

André shook his head. "No phone call yet. Maybe if we get an ID."

"*When* we get an ID," Ethan emphasized.

"I can make some calls," Hamarsson offered, "if that's what you want?"

Did André want the feds in Cooper Springs? He wasn't against their involvement; it was just that there was already a three-ring circus. Did they want to add a big top? Most likely, when it came down to it, André wouldn't have a choice.

"I've worked with the Skagit office several times," Ethan said. "It might be a bit far for them though."

Hamarsson shrugged. "They fly all over the country," he pointed out. "Go where their skills are most needed."

"Let's wait and see what we find up there," André decided.

Morrison had been so quiet during this exchange that André had almost forgotten he had an unwanted bodyguard. Two unwanted bodyguards, he revised, eyeing Bolic.

Looking around at the rest of them, Morrison patted his stomach. "Anybody else hungry?"

．　．　．

Moore, Bolic, and Hamarsson had declined the offer of a meal. Hamarsson was catching a flight back to Piedras. Ethan needed to prepare his team of three for what they were up against, and Sacha was assisting. They planned to hike up to the scene at first light the next day, map out the site, and begin retrieval. André didn't envy the hike with all the equipment they needed. If it had been summer, the team might have camped close by, but as Ned Barker had told him when he did his usual stop, weather forecasters were predicting a fierce storm was on its way. They needed to work as fast as possible and not get hurt.

André waited in the cruiser while Morrison went inside The Steam Donkey to pick up takeout for the both of them. As he'd expected, the parking lot was full. The pub was *the* place in town where everyone went for the latest gossip and, on rare occurrences, even learned something close to the truth. No way was André setting foot inside there until the hullabaloo had blown over or at least calmed down.

His radio crackled to life.

"Trespassers out near Murry Evison's property," Carol reported. "The caller said he had an encounter with an aggressive couple in an RV."

André flicked on his blue and reds but decided against the siren as he backed out of the parking spot. Another day with Deputy Cooper taking some deserved vacation time and Carol would already have tried Deputy Trent, so he must be on another call.

"I radioed Deputy Trent first. He was on the way, but then called back. His car won't start."

The state of the fleet was an issue. If André hadn't had the same thing happen when he first moved to town, he wouldn't have believed Trent. At least he'd been able to procure a new-to-him cruiser through a grant from the Department of Agriculture.

Carol rattled off an address a few miles north of town, an area that was isolated from the highway as it curved away from the ocean. There had been issues over the past year with RVers thinking the wide space in the road was a good place to stay for a few days.

It was not. It was private property owned by a very prickly and private old man.

If they were lucky, Murry would just set his dogs on them. If they weren't lucky, they might find themselves staring down the wrong end of a shotgun.

As he drove, André passed only two other vehicles, both coming from the other direction. The wind picked up as he drove, buffeting his car and causing the tops of the trees to sway back and forth. It wasn't raining yet, but he sensed big fat drops were just minutes away.

Set back from the highway and partially hidden by a canopy of cedar and pine, Murry Evison's home was a sad-looking single-wide that needed a new roof, a paint job—hell, a full remodel.

When André approached the green space next to the highway, there was no RV to be seen. Maybe the interlopers had been foolish enough to think Murry's property was abandoned and had parked near his house instead. He turned left onto the bumpy gravel drive, heading toward the structure. Fifty yards later, there was no sign of Murry's easily recognizable banged-up Jimny or an RV. Surely he wouldn't have called the station and then left his property?

Stopping in front of the house, André cracked open the car door, intending to get out, go knock on Murry's door, and find out what was going on.

It was too quiet. Even the wind had settled for the moment, and only the distant sound of waves crashing against the shore reached André's ears. Murry's three hounds were vocal and intimidating. If they were inside the house, they would have been howling and barking.

A terrible sinking feeling began to form in André's gut. What the fuck was he thinking responding to a call *alone*, in the middle of nowhere, when someone had taken a shot at him less than twenty-four hours ago?

He pulled his foot back inside and slammed the car door shut before jamming the cruiser into reverse. Pressing the accelerator hard, he reversed up the drive as fast as he dared, gravel shooting from underneath his tires as the car careened backward.

He was navigating the driveway over his shoulder when there was a sickening thunk. Risking a glance forward, André saw the windshield now had a spiderweb fracture where the bullet aimed at him had been stopped. His ballistic vest was safe in the trunk. What a fucking idiot, especially after yesterday.

If he didn't end up shot, Dante was going to finish the job himself.

Seconds later, there was another thunk. Bullet-resistant glass was only designed to withstand two or three shots, depending on the thickness. He had to get back onto the highway and hope no one was waiting to ambush him there.

"Motherfucking fucking hell."

Stomping the gas pedal to the floor, André maneuvered around the last corner onto the highway. Once there, he slammed hard on the brakes so he could change gears. Thank fuck there was no one coming from either direction. Thank fuck he'd kept up with the tactical driving courses. Thank fuck whoever was actively trying to kill him had not been waiting at the end of the drive to ambush him.

That was a mistake and André might not be so lucky next time. Three was a charm.

Shoving the gear shift into Drive, André pointed his damaged cruiser back toward Cooper Springs. There was no way he was going to be able to keep this incident quiet. Was this their suspected serial killer or something else? He wasn't any kind of profiler, but he would be surprised if someone who had been killing for years, quietly and efficiently, would suddenly start something that was loud and public.

Before reaching town, and once he got his breathing under control, André radioed Carol.

"Chief?"

"Carol, Murry wasn't there. Somebody took a shot at me, but I'm okay," he assured her. "I'm on my way back now. Reach out to Lani and Trent and tell them both to be on high alert. I think this person is only after me, but I don't want anyone hurt."

"Shot at?" her voice rose. "Did you get the bastard?"

André allowed himself one brief second to be impressed by Carol's language. The dispatcher was known to be calm, cool, and collected at all times, unflappable.

"I didn't see anyone, too busy trying to avoid the bullets."

The sign for The Steam Donkey appeared out of the mist that had rolled in off the ocean. André's stomach sank to the floor.

Triple fucking fuck. He'd abandoned his unasked-for bodyguard. There was no way the big man hadn't figured out that André had not waited in the parking lot. Which meant that Dante would also know. No. He wasn't going to stop. He'd text Dante when he figured out what his next steps would be.

Carol cleared her throat, the sound loud and intrusive.

"Your, em, friends are waiting here for you. Should I put them in the breakroom?"

Dammit.

"I'll be there in three minutes."

"Again?" Dante shouted. "You were shot at again?!"

André had parked the cruiser behind the station. In the darkness, no one would see the damage. Not right away. That was before he saw the dark figure waiting by the back entrance to the station.

"Yes. And they missed again," André replied, keeping his voice calm. He did not feel calm.

"They didn't miss," Dante hissed. "They took out your fucking goddamned windshield."

Dante had not been waiting in the breakroom, he'd been lurking outside. Looming. Furious.

And André knew he had every right to be angry.

"Look, I know. I was there. I'm going to alert the Grays County Sheriff's Office."

"And what the fuck are they going to do?" Dante demanded.

Honestly, the departments were all so short-staffed that André didn't have a clue what anyone could do, but he'd follow protocol.

"Deputy Cooper and I will head back up tomorrow and do a check on Evison's property. Carol said that his daughter-in-law told her Murry is in Arizona, so at least it wasn't him shooting at me." And the crotchety old man wasn't decomposing in his home.

"The fuck you will."

"The fuck I will," André growled. "I am not hiding somewhere and letting other people do my job."

They were chest to chest for the second time that day. This time, André wanted to wrap his fingers around Dante's neck instead of his cock. Or maybe both.

"How about you two go somewhere and fuck this out?" Morrison suggested.

André and Dante spun around to shoot death glares at the big man. They'd been so intent on each other that instead of focusing on the real matter at hand, neither had noticed Morrison opening the back door and stepping outside.

"What?"

"Excuse me?"

Morrison shrugged, not remotely phased. "Just stating the obvious. Maybe after that's out of your systems, we can focus on keeping the chief alive?" This time, his pointed stare was directed at Dante.

André clenched his jaw. Dante crossed his arms over his chest.

"No idea who could be taking shots at you?" Dante asked André, very much ignoring Morrison.

"I cannot imagine who in Cooper Springs I've pissed off enough that they want to kill me."

A rumbling sound came from Dante's chest. Making a partial fist, he began cracking his knuckles.

"*Maybe*," Morrison said with a pronounced drawl, "you boys should take this inside? If you're not going to fuck it out, I mean."

"We are not fucking anything out," Dante growled.

"This is serious, then?" Morrison waved his hand between the two of them. "That explains so much." He turned and led the way back.

"You don't think you've made an enemy in Cooper Springs. So," Morrison said as he eased himself into one of the breakroom chairs. André was learning this was a habit for him, probably after several mishaps. "What about before, as a marshal?" Morrison asked.

They both stared.

"What?" He stared back. "I checked up on you. Not letting Romeo here get involved with just anyone, am I? Plus, Hatch told me to. You're an ex-U.S. Marshal. There have to be some folks out there who would be glad to have you gone."

"I mean, you're not wrong." André sat across from Morrison. "But most of them are behind bars or dead."

"Most of them," Dante repeated. "Who isn't dead? Who is behind bars *and* has something to gain by your death?"

André tapped the top of the table. The bushes next to the only window scraped across the pane.

"I have the one case left to testify in. The date was pushed back."

"When is it? What's the case?" Dante asked.

"Aldo Campos, Mid-April."

Dante's eyes widened. "Fucking A. That was —"

A sharp, shrill sound interrupted them.

Dante shot to his feet as he simultaneously dug in his pocket for his cell phone.

"Dani, what's wrong?"

FOURTEEN

Dante

"*Zio*," Daniella breathed out her endearment for him in a voice quieter than a whisper, "I think someone's here. Outside."

Chills ran down his spine and his vision tunneled. Dante forced himself to listen, to process Dani's words. Oxygen in, out, in, and back out again.

They'd planned for this possibility. They planned for the worst, going so far as to practice together, and Dante had insisted that Daniella get comfortable locking herself into the safe room in the basement. Still, he'd hoped they would never have a reason to use it.

Dani's panicked breathing was loud in his ear.

"Are you downstairs?" he asked.

"Yes. Luna started acting weird. Like, this low growling. It scared me. I had to drag her down here with me. Zio," she sniffled, "I'm scared."

Dante was scared too. He was supposed to be there keeping Dani safe and instead, he'd allowed himself to be distracted by what was going on with André.

"Stay on the line. Don't say anything unless I speak first. Keep Luna with you."

"Okay."

Her voice was small and tiny. Dante should never have let his guard down. But he had and now he had to deal with the consequences. He'd—erroneously—assumed Dani would be fine for a few hours on her own.

He checked his watch; it wasn't late. Not even nine p.m. yet. At least the dog had been on alert. If something happened to Dani, Dante would never be able to forgive himself.

André and Morrison were on their feet—obviously, they'd figured out that something was very wrong. Morrison flipped a set of keys around his finger in a "ready already" gesture. After checking his weapon, André grabbed a CSPD jacket that had been hanging on a hook and pulled it on over his uniform. Silently, they filed out the back door of the station and into the wind and rain.

While they'd been inside, the winter storm forecasters had been warning area residents about had finally rolled ashore. The heavy thrum of the waves crashing against their strip of sand and rock set an ominous tone. Dante swore he could feel the earth vibrating under his feet. Gale-force gusts of wind whipped through the treetops while rain came down in nearly horizontal sheets.

The three of them were soaking wet within seconds. It was raining hard enough that the drops stung when they hit Dante's face. He was damp to the skin and figured Morrison and André were as well.

"No police lights or sirens," Dante said, gripping his cell phone in one hand. The connection would likely be dropped before they got to his house. Cell service was iffy at best in the county, why hadn't he invested in a sat phone?

"We're on our way, topolina, three minutes tops," Dante said quietly.

"Damn right we are," agreed Morrison before André said anything. "We'll take my car. I don't have lights."

Dante hesitated, briefly considering Morrison's car.

He was the proud owner of the self-proclaimed ugliest ride on the West Coast. Morrison maintained that the abomination, a primer-coated, matte-black Ford Taurus with varying degrees of body damage, was his secret weapon. The beast had no problem reaching 100 mph due to the engine updates he'd installed, and no one pegged it as a LEO's vehicle. That was because it looked like something a chop shop had gotten a hold of. *Frankenstein's Bad Ride.*

"Fine," Dante muttered against his better judgment. As if there was another choice. Passing the shot-up Cooper Springs police cruiser, Dante didn't allow himself to consider what had almost happened a few hours ago. André was alive, and Dani needed him now.

"Vests," André said. "I have two in the back of my car."

André jogged over to the cruiser, returning seconds later with two Kevlar vests.

"Not top of the line, but better than nothing. Sorry," he added, "neither one is big enough for you, Morrison. Don't get shot."

Without asking *why the fuck* André hadn't been wearing ballistic protection before now, Dante shrugged the offered vest on before taking the passenger seat. André donned his vest and climbed into the back. Dante peered over his shoulder when André started to speak quietly before realizing he had his cell phone pressed to his ear.

"Deputy Cooper, sorry to bother you on your day off. I'm heading out in an unmarked to a possible intrusion."

It was generous of André to describe Morrison's beast as an unmarked car.

"Yes." His tone was full of exasperation. "I have backup. Or maybe I'm the token law enforcement officer, not sure." There was a click as he secured his seat belt. "Right. Try to raise Trent as well, we might need him. I'll be in touch ASAP."

"Can you confirm your address?" André asked Dante.

"We don't need anyone else showing up." Dante forced the words through gritted teeth as Morrison sped out of the parking lot and took the first turn like he was a Formula 1 racer. Dante meant Lani Cooper, but André probably thought he was talking about Deputy Trent.

"We don't know what we'll find, Cast—Brown. Dante. We may need more firepower. Lani is a good cop and a great shot."

Dante rattled off his address and André repeated it before clocking off and tucking his phone away.

"I've got plenty of firepower in the trunk," Morrison interjected.

"I only want to know about it if it's legal," André said grimly.

"Of course, it's legal." Morrison's voice rose in semi-outrage.

"Fuck," Dante said, looking at his cell phone. "Dani's call dropped."

"You knew it was a possibility. We're almost there."

Dante appreciated that André did not assure him Dani was fine. They wouldn't know until they got there.

Morrison took another corner, faster than he had the one before. The house wasn't far now. As much as Dante wanted to mow the fuckers down, it would be better if he had as much law as possible by his side. All two of them. Two and a half, if he counted the other deputy.

"Slow down and park at the end of the block," he ordered.

"Yes, sir. Absolutely, sir. Parking right here, sir, or should we back up a few inches, sir?"

"And you wondered why Hatch keeps Morrison on a short leash."

"Actually, I hadn't wondered at all."

"How do you want to do this?" Morrison asked, ignoring Dante and André.

"Dante and I will approach the house. You stay back and watch our six. Are you good with that?" André asked.

André had his police-issue weapon, Dante reminded himself. Dante was always armed and had weapons stashed all over the house, not just in the kitchen. Morrison moved to the back of the car and popped the trunk. After rummaging around, he pulled out a twelve-gauge shotgun—very likely modified. And a stun gun.

Dante looked at him. Morrison shrugged. "If one of the bastards gets close enough, it'll slow them down and I can take them out. Sorry, I only have one set of NVGs."

A pair of night vision goggles would have been helpful.

Motioning for the other two to hurry up, Dante led the way. They silently slipped and slid along a soggy path where a sidewalk would have been if the town had installed them. Dante took the lead, then André, and Morrison was a few steps behind them.

It felt right having André by his side. André, who'd been shot at twice since just last night. André, who strode toward peril as if he expected it to bow down before him. If he was nervous, it didn't show on his face or in his walk. It made Dante curious about what had drawn him to law enforcement. Every LEO had a story. He hoped they got to share theirs.

"Car up," André said quietly.

Dante peered into the darkness, spotting the same bland, late model sedan André had—possibly the same one Dante had noticed the other day. Streetlights were far and few between on this stretch of street.

The sedan parked across and just down the street from his house wasn't anything that seemed particularly threatening, but Dante still didn't recognize it. Maybe that's why it stood out. With few exceptions, the residents of Cooper Springs drove older cars. Beaters, with rust spots and peeling paint. Cooper Springs was not a rich town; it was a barely surviving one.

"I'll cut over and check it out," Morrison murmured.

It never failed to surprise Dante how quiet and invisible Morrison could be when called for.

"Ten-four, big guy," Dante acknowledged. "Don't do anything stupid."

Morrison peeled off, a ghost crossing the street, while Dante and André continued toward Dante's rental. The wind was gusting harder now, blowing rain directly into Dante and André, and he swiped a hand across his face in a vain attempt to clear his vision. Lightning flashed mere seconds later, illuminating the area for just long enough to see the black silhouettes of leafless trees, houses, and the forest beyond.

"Let's cut through this property." Dante indicated the yard they were approaching. The house was dark, and no light peeked out around the pulled curtains. Dante knew the owners were snowbirds and had left after Thanksgiving for warmer and dryer climates.

And, yes, he had scoped out the best escape routes from the rental. While the house behind theirs had the same tiny yard, this one was on a double lot. The fence paneling at the back end was loose, and the space between boards was big enough for him and André to squeeze through. Maybe it was a good thing Morrison was checking on the sedan.

His living room lights were blazing. Dante looked away, even though his night vision was already fucked, until his eyes readjusted. For the first time since leaving the station, Dante breathed a little easier. Lights were good. Lights meant the intruders had not made it inside.

With André still at his back, Dante followed the fence to the corner of the neighbor's property and pulled the boards aside. They were being quiet, but with the storm raging, it probably wouldn't have mattered if there had been a herd of elephants wandering through the neighborhood.

Dante didn't have a plan. He had a goal and that was to get to Dani. She was hiding in the basement, in what had once been a food cellar. When he outfitted the safe room, Dante had discovered ancient home-canned fruit and what might have been pickles from back before he'd been born. It was dark and cold in there, but it was as safe as he could make it.

They hesitated in the darkest shadows on the other side of the fence. While Dante appreciated the camouflage of the storm, he wished he could see better.

André touched his arm, pointing at the back of his house.

Squinting, Dante could just make out a dark form coming around the corner opposite them. Confirmation that they hadn't gotten into the house yet.

His relief was short-lived.

A flash of something shone near the back door that was not lightning or a flashlight.

"What the fuck," Dante murmured.

"Are they trying to start a fire?" whispered André.

Fuck if that was happening. Dante and André both knew there were flammables that didn't care about the weather. He started forward, intent on getting there before disaster occurred.

A deafening explosion that outmatched the storm came from the front of the house. The figure stopped what he was doing, glancing around before straightening to his full height, then abandoned his project to dart around the house and run full speed toward the road.

"Get him!" Dante ordered as he raced across the yard to the door.

To his credit, André obeyed. He peeled off, flying after the fleeing shithead and toward the explosion. It took seconds for Dante to reach the back door, where he discovered an abandoned and mostly empty gas can and several wet rags, probably soaked with the liquid. The fabric might not have caught in this weather, but it wasn't impossible. The thought of Dani caught inside had his hours-ago lunch churning in his stomach.

He should have taken more care, but he was desperate to get

to Dani. A sound came from behind him, and Dante looked over his shoulder, thinking it was André or Morrison. It wasn't. The barrel of a gun was pointed directly at him, held firmly in the grip of a man about ten feet away. A man very comfortable with holding a deadly weapon.

"Putting you down like the pig whore you are, Castone," said the man. "Hard to miss at this range." He laughed. "I hate fucking traveling for this shit. You know how it is. Thanks for making it easy and fun for us—just a day trip."

The killer's face was almost entirely covered by a balaclava and a dark knit cap was pulled down low over his ears. Only his mouth and dark, flat eyes were exposed. Dante didn't recognize the voice, but he would never forget it.

"The girl will be next, and this job will be over. But we're gonna have a little fun with her first. Wish I could take a little more time with you too, but again, you know how this works. Time equals money and all that. I can't spend too much time enjoying myself."

A deeply disturbing grin stretched his lips wide and before Dante could react, the asshole pulled the trigger. A dim flash was followed by pain that Dante imagined was close to what it felt like being slammed directly in the chest with a sledgehammer. Clutching his vest, Dante fell to the ground, squeezing his eyes shut against the throb of agony each breath caused, but not before he spotted a looming form behind the shooter.

"I think you made a mistake," he managed to whisper.

FIFTEEN

André

"You're going to the hospital," André informed Dante.

Dante scowled and started to sit up.

"Fuck no, I am not," he groaned, easing himself back down on the slicker protecting him from the soggy ground.

"Told you so."

"Nobody likes a told-you-so. I am *not* going to the hospital. I'm fine. It just fucking hurts."

"Too fucking bad. I was shot while wearing a vest a couple of years ago. I had a bruise the size of my hand for weeks. You could have internal damage."

Arguing with Dante was obviously their love language. Arguing meant they were both alive. It so easily could have been different. They'd only just found each other. Sappy? Yes. True? Also, yes.

They'd only just found each other. André would willingly crouch in the pouring rain and argue with Dante for hours. But he wished Dante would agree to get checked out.

"I don't have internal damage. There's going to be a big fucking bruise, but I'm fine."

André allowed himself to crack a smile at Dante. He was soaking wet and filthy. His hair was plastered to his head. But his bright blue eyes blazed with determination and intelligence.

He was alive.

This situation was one of the least romantic André could possibly think of—except maybe the dentist's office—for what he was about to say. But it needed to be said. *He* needed to say it. He wasn't inviting trouble, but he had no idea what the next days would bring them.

"Dante."

"I am not going to the fucking hospital," Dante repeated.

Deputy Cooper was fifty feet away talking to a neighbor—because André wasn't above begging, and Lani had easily agreed to come in. God knew where Morrison was—ah, André's gaze found him. At the moment, he was leaning into the passenger window of the Taurus, likely talking to Dani.

"You are stubborn as a mule," André said, bringing his attention back to Dante and shaking his head. "Or maybe a camel. I've heard they're worse. Look, I get it, you're not going to the hospital. I wouldn't want to go either. That's not what I was going to say."

"Oh. What, then?"

Dante began to ease himself upward again, much slower this time. André slipped a hand around his back for an assist.

"This may seem weird but—" André shifted and huffed out a breath, not really sure how to say what he wanted to say. *Might as well just spit it out.* "Don't die on me tonight. I think—" Fuck, this was difficult. He'd never told a man he loved them before, but he was pretty sure he could do it a bit nicer. "I think I could be falling for you, Dante Castone, and I would very much appreciate you not dying as I have waited a very fucking long time for this."

Not eloquent, but he'd done it.

In spite of the pain he had to be in, a grin flashed across Dante's lips.

"You think, huh?"

"Yeah," André admitted, wishing he could kiss Dante right now. "Pretty damn sure."

The grin widened. "So, you'd be okay with me and Daniella sticking around after this shitstorm passes?"

Lightning flashed again, but further away this time, and the sky rumbled.

"I'd be very okay with that," André said. But they had to get through this shitstorm first.

Dante's dark hair was plastered to his forehead, a streak of mud ran from temple to chin, and he was wet to the skin. But the grin broadened, his teeth gleamed, and his blue eyes sparkled. He was the sexiest man André had ever known, and the only man André wanted in his life.

"Damn, I want to get started now. Let's get this situation wrapped up so we can figure the rest out. Still no hospital. I want to get naked, take a shower, and spend the night in your bed. That's a life goal in case you're curious. I'm always going to want to spend the night with you."

The rain continued to bucket down. They were both soaking and covered with mud, rotten leaves, and god knew what else, and all André wanted to do was grab Dante and hold him tight. To prove to himself that Dante was alive and well.

Fifty feet away, the smoldering wreckage of the Honda sedan's engine sparked again, sending up a tiny display of fireworks. The torrent of water falling from the sky kept the fire from spreading and, thanks to Deputy Cooper, the county's volunteer fire crew was on the way.

André was not going to ask what Morrison had done.

"Where's Dani?" Dante demanded, looking around as if someone had snatched Dani right out from under their noses. His query was followed by a loud groan as he started to stand up.

"Let me give you a hand. She and the dog are sitting with Morrison for now."

Aware that Dani had witnessed her mother's murder, André had been hesitant about exposing her to more trauma. He'd had Lani escort her to Morrison's car before they knew for certain that the vest had done its job protecting her uncle.

"I want to see her."

"If you're in such good shape, how about you get your ass over to the car instead of making your niece get soaked to the skin all over again?"

André was soaked too. They all were. He'd grabbed a second plastic slicker for himself out of Lani's trunk, but all it did was make his wet clothes feel cold and oddly sweaty.

He'd been closing in on the first intruder, but when they reached the street, the coward had seen the sedan in flames and kept running, putting on more speed and distance between them. Legs pumping, André had kept after him, but the wet clothing and water-soaked shoes slowed him down. When the intruder vaulted over a fence and disappeared, André had known it was a lost cause. After glaring at the fence, André had turned back, calling Deputy Cooper with an update as he slogged back to the scene.

Hands on his hips and lips pressed tightly together, Dante straightened to his full height.

"Stubborn."

"I'm fine."

Gingerly, Dante began slowly to make his way to the Taurus.

Shaking his head again, André moved to catch up with him. The least he could do was make sure Dante didn't fall over. That would hurt.

"Just to reiterate. I never want to go through something like that again."

When he'd returned to Dante's house, having given up the chase for perp number two, Morrison had been nowhere in sight, just the flaming car illuminated the street. Trusting that the absolute sheeting rain would keep anything else from catching fire, he'd slipped and slid his way through the churned-up grass and moss to the backyard, only to see Morrison heaving Dante up off the cold, wet ground—after he'd clocked the second intruder on the back of the head.

For a too-long horrible second, André had thought Dante was dead.

Looking up, Morrison had seen the expression on his face. "He's just stunned."

"Fucking, *fucking*, hurts," Dante had managed, confirming that he was, indeed, alive.

By the time they got back to the front of the house, Deputy Cooper had arrived, helped Dani out of the basement, and called in the emergency services. She deserved a raise.

Morrison's blow had dazed the shooter enough that André had easily been able to slap cuffs on him. He'd enjoyed it, and if they were a bit tight, so be it. The fucker had shot Dante almost point-blank, obviously intending to kill him. With one hand, Morrison had heaved him a few inches off the ground and basically dragged him face-first through the mud, around the house, and to the street while André pretended not to notice.

"Let go of me! Who the fuck do you think you are? I know my rights! My lawyer will have your badge taken away! I have friends you can't touch."

"Good luck with that seeing as how I'm not a police officer. Just a citizen lending a hand. Deputy Cooper here might be willing to listen to your complaints though," Morrison said as he effortlessly tossed the creep into the backseat of Lani's cruiser.

André had found Morrison's move impressive. The perp did not, and the mention of Lani Cooper incensed him further.

"Fuck you and fuck bitch cops," he spat, finishing up with,

"They're only good for one thing." The asshole probably would've grabbed his crotch if he wasn't handcuffed. As it was, he settled for sticking his tongue out and dragging it across his lips.

Silence swirled around them. Even the rain drops seemed to fall with quiet hesitation. Lani Cooper, all five foot six inches of her, sauntered menacingly toward the three men and their hand-cuffed prisoner sitting in the back of her car.

"Really? Would you care to elaborate further?" she asked in a tone so chilling that goose bumps immediately covered André's forearms. "Exactly what do you mean by that? What are women good for?"

From where he was standing, André saw the perp's eyes widen. A fool was born every minute.

"I didn't think so," Lani had growled. She moved closer, not saying anything, just looming larger than life as she regarded him with utter disdain. After a long moment, she shook her head and stepped back as if she'd smelled something rotten. "To think, I came back from my day off for this asshole."

"Who is the asshole anyway?" Dante asked André, having missed the part where they'd checked his ID.

"Glenn Woods. His driver's license—expired—says his home address is Miami, so he's a long way from home," André mused. "We'll learn more when we get him to the station. I'm sure he has priors."

"Glenn Woods," Dante's said slowly. "I don't recognize that name."

"If he's not grabbing a ride with us, we're taking off," called out the young first responder as he started to push the ambulance doors shut.

"Not going."

Glenn Woods was not a talker. Damn unfortunate, but it was what it was.

After reminding Woods of his rights—André figured he'd heard them many times before—the man demanded his phone call and clammed up. He was now cooling his heels in one of the station's three tiny holding cells. Generally, they were occupied by citizens who needed a nap to sleep off too much fun or some time to cool their temper down. In his short tenure, André had used it exactly twice. Woods was only his third guest.

Lani had used Carol's computer to search the record management system when they returned to the station. Glenn Woods had priors, plenty of them, but he wasn't flagged as a known associate of anyone André had dealt with. That meant absolutely nothing though. A lot of these guys were smart. After all, André and Jensen had been after Aldo Campos for months before they'd finally run him to ground. And even that had taken the help of his pissed-off ex-girlfriend.

Daniella was settled in André's office with the dog and Morrison, who she'd known from the night her mom died, according to Dante. She seemed to feel safe with him. They were alternating between watching Taylor Swift videos and listening to The Stray Kids. André appreciated the man's sacrifice.

Their situation wasn't ideal by any means, and they still needed to figure out where Dante and Daniella would be staying for the foreseeable future. Returning to the rental was not an option. Unfortunately, neither was André's house. They didn't know where the other perp had gone. He could be anywhere, and he could have fled town. André was not betting on that last one.

"What a useless human being, and I'm being generous here," Lani complained, leaning back in Carol's chair. "Morrison saw him shoot Brown point-blank."

"Maybe his lawyer will advise him to talk." André wasn't hopeful.

"Maybe pigs will fly," muttered Dante.

Thank fuck Dante had been wearing the ballistic vest when Woods had pulled the trigger. Just thinking about it made him twitchy. André shifted his stance, leaning one shoulder up against the wall of the lobby while restlessly tapping his foot. He was brimming with nervous energy.

Dante occupied one of the chairs André had dragged out of his office and was holding an ice pack against his chest every five minutes. They'd both changed into dry clothes. André kept a spare uniform at the station which he was now wearing, as well as a pair of track pants and an old training sweatshirt. Dante was wearing those.

André liked Dante wearing his clothes, even if they were a bit tight. Maybe he liked it because they were tight.

"So," Lani began, sitting forward and regarding them both with an intense gaze, "are you two planning on telling me what the hell is going on? And I don't mean the declaration Brown made yesterday."

André glanced across the room at Dante. This was his story to tell. But the more Lani knew about the situation, the better help she could be.

"Why are people trying to kill you and Chief Dear?" she asked Dante directly.

The chair creaked as Dante shifted his weight and looked up at the ceiling. Deciding what he could reveal, André supposed.

"My niece witnessed her mother's murder," Dante began. "Simone was a prosecutor with a serious caseload. The working theory is that, aside from her being able to ID the killers, they possibly think Dani knows something more—that Simone incidentally shared information. Simone's murder was likely an attempt to stop the prosecution on one of her cases, but the state isn't going to let it go. This just adds fuel to the fire for the State Attorney General's Office."

"Huh." Lani sat back again, a thoughtful expression on her face. "But that doesn't explain why somebody is taking shots at Chief Dear. Is what happened tonight related to this morning and yesterday? If not, it's an awful lot of coincidence. I'm not a fan."

"Agreed."

"So." Lani glanced over at André. "Who would shoot at you? What do you have to do with any of it?"

"Honestly, I'm not sure."

"There's a list of people mad enough they want to kill you?" She shot him a skeptical look. "Maybe you should have given that to me on your first day."

"Ha ha," grumbled André. "No list I know of. We've got a possible serial killer—I doubt he's after me. There's whoever is after Dante. Maybe Lizzy Harlow's murderer? I also don't think whoever that is would be gunning for me. And don't forget Blair Cruz is still missing, so that may be someone else too." He straightened up, one foot against the wall. "If it's tied to the Lizzy Harlow case, it's already cold. State labs are short-staffed, and I've tried to light a fire, but her case just isn't a priority." He waved a hand. "But you know all that."

"Maybe we will be a priority, now that the forensic anthropologist is here," Lani suggested.

"Maybe," André agreed doubtfully. In his experience, labs were overwhelmed and pestering them did nothing but irritate the message taker. "But other than that list, no one specific comes to mind. I haven't had any anonymous death threats or bloody fingers sent through the mail."

He thought back to the conversation they'd been having earlier before Dani had called about the intruders. It felt like days —not hours—ago.

"I'm supposed to testify in the Campos trial that's been moved to April. He was my last apprehension as a marshal. I'm just one of many involved though, definitely not pivotal to the case, and I haven't gotten word that anything's weird on my end with that one. But I suppose whoever took a shot at me could be from my marshal days."

"You helped bring Campos in?" Dante asked, lifting the ice pack to his chest again.

"Yep. That scum of a human trafficker who fancies himself the leader of a drug cartel. Seriously, did his mother not raise him better?" André wasn't a fan of the death penalty, but Campos was someone he made an exception for.

"If she was anything like mine, the answer is no."

The wind gusted powerfully outside, causing the lights to flicker, momentarily throwing the lobby in shadow.

"That's who Hatch and rest of them think put the hit on Simone," Dante said with remarkable calm. "She was the head prosecutor. Campos wasn't her only case, but he was high visibility for sure." That he could talk about Simone's death dispassionately impressed André.

"Huh," André mulled over this new-to-him information. He'd known the lead prosecutor had been killed. It had been all over the news when it happened, and they'd had to push the trial date back while they regrouped. He just hadn't put Simone Maddison and Dante Castone together. Maybe he should have, but he hadn't. In his defense, when he'd left the marshals, he'd put that life behind him and hadn't even known Dante Castone had a sister. And he'd been preoccupied with getting shot at since he'd found out Simone had been murdered, not killed in some accident.

"They have no evidence, right? Nothing to connect Campos—what a vicious piece of work—to the murder?"

"Hatch won't share everything with me. He can't. But from what he has said, they've been working under the very strong assumption that the Campos organization was behind Simone's death."

Could it be that Campos was after André too? Trying to tie up loose ends before the trial? The idea seemed fantastic, ridiculous. But if that was the case, it explained an awful lot about what was going on. And assuming the shooter was sent by Campos didn't make it any easier to stop them.

"So... This Campos guy is trying to kill two birds? Or in this case, two LEOs and a teen who witnessed her mother's murder? From behind bars. This is very Mafia, by the way," Lani mused. "Godfather-esque, even."

André would have missed Dante's reaction, only he hadn't been able to keep his eyes off him. Dante's shoulders stiffened.

"I hadn't thought of that."

A door slammed, making them all twitch. Seconds later, Morrison was standing at the end of the hallway.

"A Trojan, that's what you guys need," Morrison declared proudly.

SIXTEEN

Dante

"A Trojan *horse*," Morrison clarified. His eyes were wide and brimming with excitement as he glanced back and forth between them. "Not what you're thinking."

"What the actual fuck are you talking about? Why would we need a Trojan horse?" Dante demanded. His chest fucking hurt. He was exhausted. He *needed* five minutes alone with André. And Morrison was babbling about Trojan horses.

"Explain," said Lani.

"It makes sense, right? Your hidey-hole has been blown. You need somewhere safe until this shit is sorted out. What safer place than exactly where the assholes think you *won't* be?" He pointed a thick finger at Dante. "First thing tomorrow morning, we'll make a big show of getting you and Daniella out of town—or, even better, in a few hours." He tapped the landline sitting on Carol's desk. "Give Hatch a call and have him send up a bunch of fed cars. Anyway. You'll be seen leaving town, but you won't actu-

ally leave. You'll stay in Cooper Spring at your house. Which is a
real piece of work if you want my opinion—"

"I don't want your opinion," Dante interjected.

"Give Hatch a call."

Dante stared at Morrison, noting the confident air and the one
slightly raised eyebrow.

"You already ran this harebrained idea past him, didn't you?"

Which also meant that Hatch knew about the attempt on his
life. It wasn't as if Dante hadn't planned on looping Hatch in,
he'd just wanted to put his own spin on it.

Morrison shrugged. "Yep. You'll still have to lie low until
these guys are caught. They've got to be buzzing like pissed-off
bees. There's a reason they came after you now. Something's
afoot and we need to figure out what it is."

"Afoot? Been watching those new Poirot movies?"

A guilty expression flashed across Morrison's face. "I couldn't
handle any more Swifty sh-stuff." He glanced back down the
hallway as if Daniella was going to hear his real opinion of Taylor.

"Thanks for taking one for the team," Dante said.

Dante had listened to so much Taylor Swift in the last five
months that he knew most of the lyrics. He didn't hate her music,
but there was a limit to how many times a man could listen to
Cardigan and not start to relate to whoever she was singing about.

Suppressing a groan, Dante gingerly leaned forward and
picked up the handset—damn, the thing was fucking heavy—and
held it to his ear. The dial tone was loud and clear. That was good,
he supposed. Knowing Hatch would answer, no matter what time
of night it was—and it wasn't midnight yet—Dante pressed the
sequence of numbers he had memorized years ago.

Hatch picked up on the first ring.

"Hatch, Castone."

"Dante." Hatch's voice was hoarse; he'd probably been yelling
at people all day. Maybe all week. Hatch was one of those guys

who looked mild-mannered but when he opened his mouth, the illusion was quickly shattered.

"You're really on board with this plan of Morrison's? And I use the word plan loosely."

"It's not the worst idea he's ever had. I think it could work. We thought the Campos organization was worried about something, and this attack on you only proves us right. If you'd gone into WITSEC, this could have been avoided."

Dante did not appreciate being *I told you so*-ed every time he and Hatch spoke.

"Fuck you, Hatch. It's too late now, so quit beating a dead horse. Daniella doesn't know anything. She saw the assassins, yes, but she still can't ID them—and they're dead anyway, right?"

"Campos must think Dani knows something. And I have a theory about that."

"What?"

"Remember how I told you that what was left of two guys had been found?"

"The bodies outside of Salem?"

"Right. Well, they were a little hard to identify right away. It was the MC rags and tattoos that gave us the initial direction and tentative IDs. But funny thing that. It turns out that one of them was a known associate. Curtis Leandro, Alonso Campos's second-in-command. The other was a nobody. No significant priors. His name was Jimmy Brown—for real."

"What does that mean, that Brown was a nobody?"

"We've batted around just about every idea here in the office, and the one we keep coming back to is that Jimmy Brown was a fall guy. What if Alonso and Curtis killed Simone and Curtis maybe got twitchy, so Alonso had him taken out? And added a second just to make sure we thought both killers were dead."

"I'm out of the loop. Explain to me how Daniella would still be a threat to them if we thought the shooters were both dead."

Things were not making sense and something Lani had said

had Dante's thoughts heading another direction. He didn't want to say anything to Hatch, not until he'd confirmed a few things, but a terrible feeling of dread was blooming, and it didn't have anything to do with Aldo Campos.

"You know as well as I do that both Campos brothers are one Rorschach test this side of batshit crazy," Hatch said.

There was no denying the Campos brothers were psychopaths. So was what was left of Dante and Daniella's biological family.

"And you think we might be able to convince them that Dani and I've left town?"

If Hatch thought the plan might fool Campos, then maybe it would fool the Castones too, if it turned out the dread was right. Probably not, but Dante was done leaving his life behind him. Done lurking in the shadows. It hadn't kept Simone alive.

"If you're still not willing to go into WITSEC, it's the only plan we've got."

Right or wrong, Dante was tired of running. He'd been running for so long that he'd actually forgotten he was. He'd gotten careless, or Simone had, and it may have cost her her life. If his instincts were right, it was time for him to make a stand. Past time.

"Still not going."

And then there was André. Selfish, possibly, but Dante wasn't letting André Dear go a second time.

"Operation Trojan Horse it is."

Regardless of what he'd told Hatch, Dante had made a half-hearted effort to see if Dani would agree to go into hiding, but she'd flat-out refused. Dante wasn't forcing the issue. Especially since he didn't want to leave Cooper Springs, either.

Morrison left along with the fake convoy. His departure made Dante uneasy. As odd as he was, Morrison was a great person to have on your side. And the fact that Dani liked him was a plus.

"I'm hard to miss," he'd said. "They see me hanging around and they'll know you're still here."

He was right, but Dante didn't have to like it.

Instead of going back to the rental, Lani had offered them the keys to a house she and Forrest owned.

"It's not fancy in any way. It was our grandmother's. But we turn the heat on in the winter and make sure the raccoons haven't moved inside, leave random lights on so assholes don't break in. It's a roof over your head and most folks in town have forgotten we own it. There's sheets and blankets for the beds and the appliances work. I won't be offended if you change your mind." She shrugged, leaving the decision to them.

There was a story there and by the quirk of André's eyebrows, he didn't know it either.

"There's an alley, and you can park in the carport."

Dante accepted the keys and the directions from Lani, who was taking the night shift at the station to make sure Woods didn't disappear because fucking Trent had yet to surface. Then, under the cover of darkness, the three of them drove across the sleepy town, eventually finding themselves in a time capsule.

"This is creepy, Zio. I think it's haunted."

Dante's skin crawled. There was something about this house that was not right. He didn't exactly believe in ghosts, but this place made him reconsider.

"I think you should just come to my house. We can barricade the hell out of it." André said, glancing around at the faded orange carpet and the warped pictures hanging on the walls.

"A double-blind?" Dante asked.

He did not want to stay there. Dani was looking at him with hope in her eyes. Even the dog was quiet, huddled against her legs.

"That's what I'm thinking," agreed André. "I want to know what the fuck happened here."

"You feel it too?"

"Hell yeah. And I don't want to stay a second longer."

Decision made, they left the same way they'd arrived. Out the backdoor—locking it behind them—and leaving the house exactly as they'd found it. They hadn't made it past the living room.

"You're sure this is a good idea?" André asked. "We don't know what we could be walking into at my place. But maybe whoever it is hasn't found my home address? I was only targeted at the station and out by Evison's place."

"There's only one way to find out," Dante said through clenched teeth. "When we get there, Dani, you stay in the car with Luna. André and I will check the house and make sure it's all clear."

"We don't have to do this, Dante. We can drive into Aberdeen and stash you in a Motel 6."

"Dani? What do you want?"

"I want this over with. I want a normal life. I'm tired of being scared all the time, and I don't think I'll be less scared at a hotel."

"Okay, my place it is."

"I want to know what the story is behind that house."

"Or maybe you don't."

"Maybe I don't."

"I'll let Lani know we've changed our minds. She said she wouldn't be offended."

While Dani and Luna had waited in the car, André and Dante had made sure no one was hiding out, ready to ambush them inside the house. There'd been no sign of a break-in or tampering, no footprints in the grass, so they all congregated in the living room.

"Dani, how about you and Luna take the spare room?" André said. "Sorry I haven't spent a lot of time making it into a guest room or anything. That's what happens when you don't have family to show up unexpectedly."

Motioning for them to follow, André led the way down the

hall to the cluttered room across from what Dante knew was André's bedroom. Inside was a futon-style couch with a couple of pillows stacked on it. There were also weights and a treadmill that André pushed to the side.

"It should do until your uncle and I get everything sorted out. Do you want some hot chocolate or something before you go to sleep?"

Dani shook her head.

"Okay, I'll be in the kitchen if you need anything."

André stepped out of the room, pulling the door closed behind him.

"Tomorrow we'll get toothbrushes and stuff like that, okay?"

Dani nodded. "And dog food."

"And dog food. You make yourself comfortable."

"Do you think André will mind if Luna sleeps with me on the bed?"

"If he does, we'll buy him a new one. But I doubt he minds."

"Okay."

Dante pulled the blankets back and patted the futon. "Get in and try to sleep."

Dani crawled onto the bed and lay down. The dog didn't hesitate, getting right up and snuggling into Dani's side.

"I love you, Zio."

"I love you too, topolina."

Bending down, Dante kissed his precious niece on the forehead and silently vowed to protect her with his life before leaving the room.

"How's she doing?" asked André.

"Traumatized and freaking out but trying to hide it."

"I'm sorry."

"Why are you sorry? This isn't your fault."

"Eh." He shrugged. "Do you want hot chocolate?"

Dante smiled to himself. Cooper Springs was André's town—he felt responsible for what happened to its citizens. They'd never talked much, true, but Dante *knew* André. He was a damn good man.

"Sure, why not? It isn't as if I'm going to sleep."

He watched as André poured milk into a silver container, set it in onto a base, and pressed a button. A green light lit up and the machine began to whirr quietly while André spooned chocolate mix into two mugs.

"What's that?"

"A milk warmer," André said proudly. "I use it for, well, obviously hot chocolate, but it's also great for lattes too."

"Always surprising me, aren't you?"

Dante was avoiding bringing up what he needed to bring up, the idea that Lani Cooper had sparked back in the station. He did not want to. Talking about his family was low on Dante's list of Fun Conversational Gambits. Except, of course, for Simone and Daniella.

He sucked in a breath and ripped off the proverbial bandage.

"Back at the station, Lani got me thinking about everything that's been going on."

André turned to face him, leaning against the edge of the counter. "What?"

"So, look, this isn't something I'm proud of, which is why I never talk about it. My family, the Castones, are *Family*."

"What do you mean by family?" Comprehension dawned. "Oh, you mean *Family*, like capitalized, as in the Mafia. The Mob."

"That, unfortunately, is exactly what I mean. Trust me, I was never a part of the life. I was the youngest of too many brothers and sisters, and Simone was the next oldest. At least two of them died before I was born, and Simone and I were always tight. Simone got herself a scholarship and was gone before I graduated. Then she put herself through law school—so fucking smart. Once I got out here, I did a criminal justice program and that was that.

As far as I know, neither of us ever spoke to any of our other relatives again."

The warmer beeped and André grabbed it, pouring milk into each of the mugs, then set the carafe down again and stirred in the chocolate. Then he put the full cups on the table and sat down across from Dante.

"Keep talking."

"Campos is a psycho, you're right about that. He's a cold-blooded asshole with no regard for human life."

André nodded his agreement.

"But so is my oldest brother. He may be even worse. When Lani made that comment about the Mafia, it got me thinking about the Family. What's happening is eerily similar to what happens when they decide they're better off with you dead."

"Why would they, or your brother, come after you now though? What does he have to gain from killing Simone?"

"Lu doesn't have anything to gain. But gain doesn't mean anything to him. I'm guessing here because, like I said, I put them out of my mind. My grandfather was the only one who could keep Lu in line. He must be dead by now.

"Luigi always hated me. I don't know why. I just learned early on to stay out of his way. Once, when I was in high school, he tried to kill me. I was crossing the street and saw his car down the road. He looked right at me and pressed on the gas pedal. When I got home, I thought maybe he'd laugh it off, tell me his foot had slipped or some shit. He looked right at me and drew a finger across his throat."

André didn't say anything, just sipped his chocolate and waited for Dante to keep talking.

"I never slept at home again. Couch-surfed the rest of senior year. Graduated, bought a cheap car, drove to the West Coast, made a new life for myself."

"You've been undercover for most of your career," André

mused. "If your family wanted to find you, it would have been difficult."

This was also true. Dante had never owned a home or had a car loan. There was no Facebook or any other social media. His life was not lived where other people could randomly peek into it.

"He hated Simone too. But that's because Luigi hates all women. And because she was smarter than him."

André narrowed his eyes and nibbled at the inside of his mouth. "I have to ask. Is there an underlying cause for this behavior by your brother? Was your house... not safe?"

Dante snorted. "It wasn't safe, but not for the reason you're implying. My dad was second to my grandfather. Dad was sent up around the same time the Gottis were, so we ended up living with Pops. Pops was then caught up in some gambling bullshit and likely helped hide more than a few bodies, so he's got a few more years. Lu liked to brag that they all played cards together— him, Pops, the Gottis. Maybe it's true, maybe not. But no, he wasn't beaten or forced to play the piano for hours without going to the bathroom. He's a natural-born psycho."

"I'm still not convinced this isn't Campos."

"Hatch told me something else," Dante said.

"Yeah?"

"He sent the DEA compatriot in—Jensen, who was on the apprehension team as well—to talk to Aldo after Simone died. Under the guise of the whole 'maybe it's time you gave us some information we can use' argument. The guy is smart, so of course he didn't reveal anything. Not until Jensen was getting up to leave. Then he said, 'The prosecutor was snuffed, and she had a kid? I'd like to pay my respects, maybe send some flowers along with my thoughts and prayers.' Creepy as fuck, yes. As revolting a human being as Campos is, Jensen said it felt like he was genuinely shocked that Jensen would think he had anything to do with her death."

"But that was months ago. And psycho."

Dante nodded. "It was months ago, yes. Hatch didn't tell me until recently. But he's been thinking, and this time he visited Aldo himself. Aldo is a difficult read, one of those who seems to get more information from the interviewer than the other way around."

André sipped his hot chocolate, his eyes on Dante.

"Aldo asked to leave and, on his way out, he said, 'I don't threaten children.'"

André snorted chocolate up his nose, and Dante rose to bang him on the back. But André waved him off, wiping the liquid off his face with a napkin.

"Exactly my response," agreed Dante. "Well, maybe not hot chocolate up my nose. Aldo has rules known only to himself, and possibly his brother, that he follows —which people he considers human vs. which are inventory. Simone was an adversary and a woman, but she was smart, and I think he enjoyed sparring with her."

"So, you think it wasn't Campos who sent the killers?"

"*Maybe* it wasn't, maybe he's just lying through his teeth to fuck with us." Dante ran his hands through his hair. "There just seems to be so much going on, and the fucker who shot me tonight used the phrase *pig whore*."

"Okaay, so that's creative and also excessive."

"I admit, it's something I haven't heard in a while. He used English, but it's more common in Italian—*Porca Puttana*, pig whore. It was Lu's two favorite words when we were kids. The more I think about it, the more I wonder if the two at the house tonight were sent by my loving older brother."

"Woods is not an Italian name. And while dick face is creative, anyone could use it."

"Meh, Woods's family name doesn't matter these days, which I'm sure you know. I'm curious to see who shows up to represent him. I think then we'll have a better idea of who hired him."

"I'm pissed the other guy got away," André said as he got up, rinsed out his cup, and set it in the sink. "He was fast and seemed to know where he was headed. The exploding sedan didn't faze him."

Dante finished his drink and brought the cup over to André. Suddenly, he was exhausted. The stove clock claimed it was almost two in the morning.

"Let's go lay down for a while," he said, running his hand down André's strong back and letting it rest at the top of his ass.

A little grin twitched Dante's lips as André turned off the water and turned to him.

"Are we shutting our eyes? It's been a long-ass day, and we don't know who's out there."

"I think we'll be fine for a few hours, but I don't plan on resting." Whoever was after them had their work cut out for them.

Dante slipped a finger into the belt loops of André's slacks, tugging him close enough that their foreheads touched.

"I want to take you to bed. I need to feel you against me—selfish, I know."

André's hand lifted to rest against Dante's cheek. His fingers were warm, and he drew them around and underneath Dante's chin, holding him still.

"I think we can manage that," André whispered, closing the last inch and pressing his lips against Dante's.

SEVENTEEN

André

The wind howled, rattling the window and doors in their frames, and the pounding rain hadn't let up, but André had Dante in his bed. The storm couldn't reach them, not for a few hours anyway. Between the two of them and Luna, they would keep Daniella safe. He should've headed back to the station, but he couldn't make himself. He had a visceral need to make sure Dante and Dani were safe.

He needed this. They both needed this.

Dante had almost died—would have died if he hadn't been wearing the vest—and André's lonely life had flashed before his eyes. The worst had almost happened. They had dangerous jobs and there was always a chance of one of them not coming home. But it was a risk André was willing to take.

"I want to tell you something about my past."

They'd stripped without turning on the bedside lamp. But that only meant that the diffuse glow from the streetlight limned

Dante's form, accentuating his natural muscle, his deep chest, the strong lines of his shoulders. André was planning on mapping out every dip and curve of him.

Before they got busy, André retrieved the lube from the bedside table. He ignored the box of condoms.

"Now?" Dante traced a finger around André's bare nipple before heading downward toward his bobbing erection.

"Tonight. Or before we get up again, anyway."

"Okay," Dante agreed, gently nudging him toward the bed.

Smiling, André crawled onto the mattress and positioned himself on his back. Over the course of their time together, they'd switched things up. But if he was being honest, he generally preferred it when Dante took charge.

"Fuck me." Not a question.

"Damn fucking straight," Dante declared. "Or not."

He wasn't sure what he'd expected, but it wasn't supreme gentleness. Dante slipped under the covers next to André, tucking himself in close. In the warm dark, they began to run their hands down, across, and over each other's bodies as if relearning each other.

Remembering what it felt like to be loved.

Dante brushed calloused fingers over André's nipples before licking and sucking one and then moving on to the other. André was a nipple man. He arched into Dante, silently begging for more. The only thing keeping him quiet was Daniella in the room across the hall.

"Mmm, you like that," whispered his lover.

His cock was leaking onto his stomach. Dante's fingers found the liquid and traced through the dampness, somehow managing not to touch him. André arched his back again, seeking more— being touched, caressed he was dry earth soaking up the first rainfall.

Lightning flashed, illuminating the room. Dante threw off the covers and moved down André's body with intent. André's fingers scrabbled at the sheet as Dante took him into his mouth. He did his best not to jam his cock down Dante's throat. Instead, he tried to relax, to let himself float on the river of sensation.

Dante's head bobbed as he sucked and released. As he took André's cock further down his throat. As he drove André fucking wild with want.

With a trembling hand, André reached down to run his palm across Dante's head, his fingers tangling in his hair. His balls were tight already. It would be so easy for him to come. He tapped Dante's ear.

"I don't want to come like this, not tonight." That fact he was able to form a coherent thought, much less speak, was a miracle. "Let me turn over."

Releasing André's cock and letting it slip from between his lips, Dante shook his head.

"Like this. You on your back."

They'd never done that before. It would have been too much of a commitment, too much open emotion between them.

"Okay. No condom though unless we need one. I'm negative."

"Last test in August, negative."

André had only had sex without a condom twice in his life. The first time was when he was a careless twenty-year-old who'd then spent the next year panicking that he'd exposed himself to HIV. The second was with someone he'd thought he loved. Chad hadn't been able to understand why André wanted to be a marshal, and he hadn't missed Chad much after he moved out.

This was different.

Dante rose onto his hands and knees to stare down at André. His cock hung low and full, and André's ass twitched with anticipation. Reaching up, he traced its outline with his finger and was rewarded with a pulse of precome, a full-body shiver, and a low growl.

"What you do to me, André."

Because he wanted to feel the silky hardness of him in his

hand, André wrapped his fingers around Dante's erection, gently pumping a few times. Dante threw his head back, chest rumbling as he suppressed a second, longer growl. His lips curved upward, and he batted André's hand away and scooted backward. Strong hands landed on André's hips, and he pulled him up onto his thighs.

"I need to get you ready."

Leaning to the side, Dante grabbed the lube from where it lay and squeezed some onto his fingers.

"I'd eat you out, but I don't think either one of us could be quiet."

André's balls tightened at his words and more precome oozed from his cock. They'd never done that either. There was so much to look forward to.

"Spread your legs."

Another crack of lightning and for a second, André got to see as Dante reached down between them and smoothed the cool lube over and around André's entrance. This time it was André who threw his head back and clutched the sheets. Dante chuckled.

"I almost forgot how much you like this."

Dante worked agonizingly slowly. Tracing André's hole with his finger, massaging the lube into the sensitive skin.

"Dante," André begged.

Serious now, Dante began pushing his finger inside of André, past the reluctant ring of muscle. André bore down, welcoming the thick digit into his body. They were trying to be quiet, but André could hear himself breathing, panting, *needing*.

"Another?"

André nodded, beads of sweat dripping down his forehead.

Dante complied, carefully removing the one finger and then beginning again with two. The almost-pain was exquisite, and André's cock hardened further—or maybe it was his balls. He was nothing but sensation as Dante's digits worked their magic.

When they began to scrape across André's prostate, he grabbed his cock in desperation, gripping it hard to keep himself from coming.

"Dante," he said through gritted teeth. "You. In. Me."

"Yeah," Dante panted. "That."

With a tenderness that always surprised André, Dante pulled his fingers out of André's ass. André breathed in as Dante's cock began to take their place. Dante didn't have a monster cock—thank god—but he wasn't small either. After what felt like hours, he eased his thick, rock-solid erection across André's prostate.

"This is incredible. You are incredible."

Spreading his legs as wide as possible, André gave up trying to keep himself from coming. It was clear Dante was on board as well. Their hips pistoned in an age-old dance, mirroring each other while Dante's dick went back and forth, hammering André's prostate. André's impossibly hard cock throbbed every time Dante bent closer or it brushed against his body.

It was Dante who broke first.

"Shit, André. I can't stop."

"Don't you fucking dare."

Reaching underneath André's hips, Dante jammed himself as far into André's hole as was humanly possible. André wrapped his legs around his waist, holding him in. Warm come filled his hole as Dante pulsed inside of him.

"Jesus Fucking Christ," Dante whispered, his hips stuttering as he continued to come.

André arched his back instinctively. He needed just a little more contact. He was so close.

Returning to himself, Dante reached out and gently ran his index finger around the mushroom-shaped cap of André's penis. His touch felt like fire, sending sparks from André's hole up his spine.

"Come with me inside?" Dante asked.

The sound André made in return wasn't a human one. But

Dante must have realized a few tight touches were all he needed. He proceeded to wrap his hand around André and pump once and then again. André's entire body jerked and jolted. His already tight balls released and come erupted from his tip, spilling over his stomach and onto the sheet.

Dante kept pumping until André's sac was empty and he whimpered.

"Good, I'm good."

"Fuck, me too.'

"I know all the books make it clear I'm not supposed to confess that I love you immediately after sex. But I do." André breathed deeply.

"Screw what all the books say," Dante said as he slowly pulled his cock out of André's body. "I love you too. Don't get up. I'll grab something to clean us up."

Dante left the bedroom and André just lay there, unable to move. Partly because his shoulder was stiff but mostly because what they'd just done had been incredible.

A minute later, Dante was back with a warm washcloth. After wiping André down, he tossed the cloth into the clothes hamper and climbed back underneath the covers.

"We should probably change the sheets."

"Yeah, well, we'll be getting up very soon, so I'm not going to worry about it. What did you want to tell me? Before?"

Right. André had felt the need to share one of the deepest, darkest truths about his past. He knew it was important that Dante know but it was a source of shame, a part of his life where André had failed.

"Ugh."

"Just get it out now, in the dark. It's easier. You're not a serial killer? Or worse?"

"No. It's about my family."

"Cannot be worse than mine."

"Maybe not worse, but equally terrible."

"Okay, spill."

"I grew up in Ohio."

"Oh, damn, André. Ohio is a terrible secret."

"Fuck you." André poked Dante in the ribs. "I grew up in Granville, not big, not super small. Around twenty-five thousand residents."

"That's pretty small," Dante conceded, grabbing André's hand and keeping it against his side.

"My dad was on the police force. He was an asshole—but, of course, I didn't really know that until I was older. My mom got fed up with him, with having two kids, and left when I was almost six. Understandably, I was angry she deserted us like that. But she was very young with very little education, and her family all lived in Canada. As far as I know, that's where she went. For a short time after that we—my brother and I—had a string of also very young women who wanted to take care of two motherless boys and a wifeless man, until good old Dad showed his real self, then they'd leave.

"By the time I was in high school, I'd realized it wasn't Mom, it wasn't us, it was him. I sucked it up, waiting to graduate—kind of like you did. I finished high school and have never been back to Granville."

"And your brother?"

"Gene. We were only eighteen months apart. But he never left town like I did. He and Dad just lived in that same house together. When I was twenty-two, Gene shot our dad. Before he turned the gun on himself, he drove around town and took three other innocent people's lives."

"André." Dante rolled onto his side. He slipped his arms around André, holding him tight and stroking his hair. Comforting him in a way André had never been comforted. "That's terrible," he whispered against his forehead. "You must have felt so guilty. It wasn't your fault. You weren't there. You aren't your father or brother."

These were things André had told himself repeatedly over the years. He'd been to therapy, more than once. And that didn't include the counselor the Marshals Service had required when they learned of his past. Dante's touches and words were a salve he hadn't known he wanted. Needed.

"Mostly, it's just a memory. But I didn't want it to be a secret between us. I'm not ashamed, not anymore. I do feel guilty for leaving Gene on his own."

"We both carry burdens. Family can suck. And you'll never know what was going on inside your brother's head."

André managed a nod. "True. I have wondered if our mother ever saw the news on TV."

He liked having Dante wrapped around him. He wasn't looking forward to the arrival of morning. Here in the dark, sharing the warm covers with Dante, he felt safe. The world was on pause, but André knew it was an illusion and tomorrow they would have to put their literal and figurative armor back on and figure out what the hell was going on.

As if he'd heard André's thoughts, Dante said, "Once we get whatever the fuck is happening sorted out, we should take a vacation together."

André yawned. "Maybe we should try and grab some shut-eye first. I set an alarm for six. Gotta get to the station and relieve Lani from perp watch. The lawyer said they'd be here first thing too."

"No rest for the wicked," Dante mumbled.

"None at all. Hey."

"What?" Dante rolled onto his back.

André couldn't see the bruise in the darkness, but he knew exactly where it was. Skating a hand across Dante's chest, he gently traced along the purple mark. "You scared me today. Let's try not to do that again."

Again, Dante grabbed his hand and pressed it against his chest, directly over his heart. André slipped into an uneasy slumber where he dreamed masked intruders were trying to get at Dante and Daniella and he was the only person keeping them safe.

Six a.m. came far too soon. The sun was still hanging out in the southern hemisphere and, while the storm had let up some, the winds and rain continued to howl and pelt.

Sleep had not been restful, but it had been satisfying to lie in the bed for a few hours with Dante's warm body next to his. It would be even better when he figured out who was after them. Was it one faction or two different contingents? Was it someone from town or someone from their collective pasts?

Rolling onto his side, André pulled the covers back, doing his best not to disturb his bed partner.

"Is it time?" Dante asked. He didn't sound as if he'd been asleep either.

"Yep. I'm going to make some coffee and check in with Lani."

After slipping into sweats and a t-shirt, he stepped into the hall. The dog was snuffling at the bottom of the door to the spare room. As quietly as possible, he turned the knob and pushed it partway open. Luna came shooting out and headed directly for the kitchen. André's gaze landed on Dani. The teen was asleep, curled up around one of the pillows with the covers pulled up to her nose. It would do her good to sleep as long as possible. Who knew how long it would be before they all slept well again.

Peering out into the dark, André noted that the wind and rain had indeed dialed it down a bit at some point in the last few hours. Unlocking the kitchen door, he let the dog out. She raced to one corner and peed before darting back and forth for a few minutes, sniffing and snuffling. Small animals often ran through his backyard on their way to trees and burrows, and Luna was clearly enjoying tracing their movements.

"Luna, get back inside."

The dog turned and looked over her shoulder at him, a decidedly contemplative expression on her face, as if considering whether she would come or not.

"Come on, get your furry butt inside."

With a defiant last sniff at a random clump of grass, Luna reluctantly made her way back to André.

"Good girl. We'll get you breakfast as soon as we can." As she slipped past him into the house, André dried her off with a kitchen towel.

"I guess I'm going to have to do laundry at some point." He hung the damp towel on the door handle for the time being.

Soft footsteps sounded behind him. Turning, he saw Dante coming toward him.

"What's the plan?" Dante asked, moving further into the kitchen. His hair was damp, so he'd had a quick shower, and he was already fully dressed. André was disappointed he'd missed naked shower time.

"Make coffee. Head to the station and touch base with Lani. Track Trent down. With everything going on around here, I don't appreciate whatever game he's been playing."

"Oh, yeah? I knew he was an issue. What's his deal?" Dante started to lower himself into one of the chairs but stood up again, obviously too restless to sit.

André grabbed pods for his espresso machine from the cupboard and lined up two of the many to-go mugs he kept on hand. He probably had more cups with lids than regular ones. Thinking about the day ahead of them, he grabbed two more coffee pods. They were going to need double shots to start their day.

"He's a relic I inherited when I accepted the job. I've done what I can to remove him from as much forward-facing police business as possible." André dropped a pod in, set one of the cups underneath the nozzle, and pressed the magic button. "Unfortunately, he complained to the union. So, I've been sending him and Lani to as many courses as the department can afford to try and bring him up to speed, both as an officer and human being. Which so far has been two."

"Has it helped?"

"Nope. He continues to act as if the town is supposed to appreciate his thirty-five years on the force, during which his greatest achievement has been to *not* be sued by the high number of women and minorities he's handed out various tickets to over the years. As if we owe him something."

André thought about the spreadsheet he'd put together and shook his head.

"You were there when I learned purely by chance that he did nothing when Xavier Stone was set up and beaten by his supposed date. That was over twenty years ago, but Trent hasn't changed much since then. I've also heard through the grapevine that he was very unhappy when Mayor Moore chose to hire from the outside instead of promoting him to the chief's position."

"What a lovely person to have representing the Cooper Springs PD. Deputy Cooper seems much better qualified."

"My thoughts exactly. And you're right, Lani would make a good chief. But she doesn't want the job."

André handed Dante the first cup of coffee and then made his own.

"I'm going to take a quick shower too, then I'll be ready to go."

"I'll get Dani up."

Grabbing his coffee and following Dante, André veered into the bathroom and took a quick shower, not bothering to shave. Cooper Springs would just have to deal with a scruffy police chief. Returning to his bedroom, he pulled on blue jeans instead of slacks, then a t-shirt, then a thick CSPD sweatshirt over that. If things kept going sideways like this, he was going to have to invest in a few more uniforms.

Dani and Dante were waiting in the living room for him when he emerged.

"Ready?" he asked and received two nods in response.

As they'd expected, Glenn Woods refused to answer any questions when his lawyer arrived. The defense attorney, Bradley Cooper—no relation—requested that his client be transferred to a "more humane" holding cell in Aberdeen while they waited for the judge to rule on bail. That request had been easy to agree to. For the time being, he was being held as a flight risk. Miami was a long way from Cooper Springs.

André spoke with the Grays County prosecutor on the phone. Tillotson agreed to have Woods moved to Aberdeen, and at just after nine a.m., he and Lani Cooper were watching a Grays County sheriff's vehicle head south with Woods in the backseat.

"That's one down," said Lani. "And good riddance. He made my skin crawl."

André wholeheartedly agreed.

"Have we heard from Deputy Trent yet this morning?" he asked Lani.

"No. I had Carol call him when she arrived, but he didn't answer and hasn't called back yet."

"Dammit." André had hoped to avoid driving to Trent's home and rousting him out of his nest. But it seemed the man was going to force him to do just that. He dragged on his Kevlar vest. André didn't believe Trent was the shooter, but he was going to be careful.

If the shooter had been Woods—*my client has nothing to say*—André was in the clear. If the shooter was the second perp—*my client has no comment*—then he could still be in danger. The now dark purple bruise on Dante's chest was a reminder of just how close he'd come to losing him.

As bulky and unwieldy as the Kevlar was, André didn't plan

on being a statistic because of vanity. There was still the chance that André's shooter wasn't related to what was going on with Dante and Daniella, but André had always subscribed to the simple solution first. If it barked like a dog, it was a dog.

"Would you like me to go along?" Lani asked.

"No. We both know Trent won't take a visit from you well at all. I'll do it."

He wanted Lani to stay back with Carol and Dani. A person would have to be out of their mind to break into a police station, but he wasn't taking any chances.

"Consider having Dante go along for the ride then," Lani suggested. "Carol and I will keep Dani safe."

André pressed the doorbell, but there was no resounding chime from inside the house. The wind buffeted against his back. It was picking up again, a second storm rolling in off the Pacific, and really, he'd rather not get soaked two days in a row. Pressing his thumb hard against the button again in case there was a bad connection, he listened for a chime. Nothing. He tried peeking in through the blinds, but they were drawn tight.

Trent's house was not what he expected. He'd expected a run-down double-wide or a post-war cottage that needed work. Instead, Trent lived in a cozy, two-story, wood-and-brick house with a tidy front lawn. Colorful garden gnomes with watchful eyes were observing them from underneath leafless hydrangea bushes.

"Is it just me, or is this place a little disturbing?" Dante asked from where he was waiting by the bottom step. The small porch wasn't big enough for both of them, and he'd insisted on coming even though there wasn't another vest for him to wear. "This one is better than nothing," he'd said.

André supposed he wasn't wrong. The damaged vest *was* better than no vest, but he didn't like it.

"Very disturbing. It's the gnomes, they're watching us."

Raising his fist, André banged against the front door, rattling it in the frame. He smiled to himself; it had been a while since he'd gotten to use his marshal's knock.

"Trent, you in there?"

He was about to knock again when he heard a rustling sound and then slow footsteps approaching the door.

"Just a dammed second," a voice grumbled.

The door opened about halfway, and André found himself almost eye to eye with a late-middle-aged person wrapped up in an ancient plaid bathrobe.

"Good morning, I'm Chief André Dear. We're looking for Lionel Trent."

"Oh, I'm Lionel's sister, Chief Dear." Turning her head slightly, the woman coughed into her fist. When she got her breath, she straightened up again, her curious beady gaze pinging from André to Dante waiting on the walkway and back again.

"Is Lionel home? We've been trying to reach him, but he hasn't responded."

The woman contemplated André, her expression reminding him of Luna's when she was trying to decide whether to come inside. The wind gusted again, driving sharp drops of rain against the back of André's neck and causing the woman's bathrobe to billow. She narrowed the opening further, trying to keep the heat inside and the wind out.

"I haven't seen my brother in a day or so." She didn't sound particularly worried about Trent's whereabouts. "I have to say, he doesn't have a very high opinion of you, Chief Dear."

André hadn't known that Trent's sister was living with him. Or maybe it was the other way around. He didn't know much about Trent at all. He hadn't even known Trent had a sister. And he couldn't care less what Trent's opinion of him was.

"Do you mind if we come in and ask you a few questions?"

The sister didn't immediately step back, but she didn't say no. "I've had the flu, so enter at your own risk."

André eyed Trent's sister, cataloging her appearance. She did seem a bit pale, and she certainly hadn't brushed her short, graying hair that morning. But then, André hadn't bothered to shave, so perhaps he was being a tad judgmental.

"I'm sorry to hear that," André said, deciding against stepping inside. "Lionel hasn't returned our phone calls, so we're concerned. When you see your brother, would you let him know to contact us?"

The woman shivered, tightened her bathrobe around herself, and moved enough so she was effectively blocking André's view of the living room.

"I 'spose. Like I said, I haven't seen him in a few days."

"Thank you, we appreciate your assistance." André nodded encouragingly. Pulling out his wallet, he handed her a business card. "Here's my direct number. If you think of anything, or if you hear from your brother, please give me a call."

She held the card between two fingers as if it was something disgusting, not merely a piece of cardstock.

Turning away, he took the three steps to the yard and the door shut behind him with an audible bang. The space between his shoulder blades twitched, and André moved faster. He didn't like having his back to Trent's home.

"Let's go."

"Ten-four," Dante said, opening the passenger door and climbing inside.

André flipped on the windshield wipers and pulled the car out into the street. There wasn't much traffic, but then there never was in Cooper Springs. Traffic was one of those things that happened somewhere else.

"How long are you and Deputy Cooper going to have to share a cruiser?" Dante asked.

"Fucking hell." André slammed his hand against the steering

wheel. "I haven't brought the mayor up to date." He hadn't seen or spoken with Roslyn Moore since the news conference—yesterday? The day before? Fucking hell.

"There's been a lot going on. I'm sure she'll understand."

"I fucking hope so."

EIGHTEEN

Dante

Understandably frustrated, André stomped back to his office to call the mayor as soon as they arrived back at the station. Dante said hi to Carol before wandering back to the breakroom where Dani was playing a card game with Lani. Luna hopped up to greet him with a tongue swipe and cold nose.

"I don't have anything for you," he informed the dog.

"Hi, Zio," Dani said, not looking up from her hand.

"Hey, topolina, how's it going?"

"I'm pretty sure you know how it's going."

"Yeah, I do," he replied, squeezing her shoulder. "With any luck, this is going to be over soon." His chest throbbed, a constant reminder that they were still smack in the middle of the shitstorm, but he couldn't sit at the station and do nothing. That was not how Dante Castone operated.

"I hope we have a lot of luck." Dani stared at her cards before laying down a five of spades.

Lani laid her cards down on the table with a sigh. "You win again. This is not good for my ego." She looked over at Dante standing in the doorway. "I want to take a drive around the neighborhood. The fact that we still haven't caught up with the second perp from last night is troubling."

The perp that got away bothered Dante a lot. He, or she, seemed to have vanished into thin air. No one Lani had talked to during her canvas of the neighborhood had seen or heard anything—they'd all been distracted by the flaming Honda. Thank you very much, Morrison.

"They could have had a car stashed somewhere."

"Yup, and in that case, they might be long gone. I'm still going to take a drive around town." Lani stood up from the table. "They could be hiding out."

"How about I ride along with you?" Dante offered.

Dani would be safe with André in the building.

"Are you okay with me going out again?" he asked his niece.

She looked up from where she was laying out a hand of solitaire. "Yeah. I just want this to be over, Zio. I'd also really appreciate it if you didn't get shot this time."

Daniella looked and sounded so much like Simone that it made Dante's heart ache. He missed his sister with an almost overwhelming ferocity. He didn't plan on letting Dani down. If anyone was going to be shooting anyone, it would be Dante aiming at the asshole who was after them.

"I'll do my best, topolina. Well?" He directed that to Deputy Cooper.

"Sure. Run it past the boss first though. And wear a vest."

Dante tapped lightly on André's office door before pushing it open.

"I'm headed out with Cooper to do a drive around," he said softly.

André nodded, holding his phone's handset against his ear as he listened to the mayor and jotted some notes down. Or maybe he was doodling. Dante resisted the urge to kiss him on the neck, but he wanted to. André must have read the expression on his face because the corners of his lips turned up and he nodded again before waving him away.

Lani was waiting for him in the lot behind the building. Dante slid into the passenger seat.

"Vest on, got my Glock too." He patted his holster. "I'm good to go."

"Alright, let's do this."

Dante had a weird feeling in the pit of his stomach. There was no other way to describe it. The calm before the storm, tranquility before chaos. Something had to give. Something was going to happen, and soon. Whoever was gunning for him and Dani, or him and Dani and André, wasn't going to wait around while they recircled the wagons. They'd proven that last night.

"What's up with that house?" Dante found himself asking as Deputy Cooper took a right onto the street. "Was that a test to see if we'd stay in a haunted house? Not that I believe in ghosts or anything."

The corner of Lani's mouth quirked upward. "Oh, it's haunted all right. Or maybe possessed. I have my theories and Forrest has his. But it wasn't a test, I just thought you might hide out there, for a night anyway."

She'd known they wouldn't, but that was beside the point.

"Well, what's your theory?" Dante wanted to know.

"It belonged to our maternal grandparents. Jerry and Norma Paulson. My grandfather died very young, and Norma never remarried."

She took another turn, taking them along meandering streets that would eventually end up close to Dante's rental.

"It was just Norma and our mother in the house. Norma fancied herself a healer, a witch of sorts. She'd take Dina into the woods for days at a time, collecting the things she needed. Dina pretty much grew up in the forest. I learned all this from my paternal grandfather, mind you, so there's probably some bias. He and Norma didn't get along."

"That could be a good thing, growing up in the woods," Dante said tentatively. There was obviously a story here and he wanted to hear it.

"Well, yes, it *could* be. Who knows? Was Norma mentally ill? Was it something else? Did she accidentally ingest something fatal? Anyway, Norma died in that house, possibly by her own hand. The town mythos is that she couldn't live without her husband any longer. I don't know about that. It'd been something like fifteen years by that point." They turned another corner.

"Dina couldn't stand to live in the house without her mother, and supposedly her mother came to her in a dream and told her to get out. She convinced her boyfriend, Witt Cooper, to get married and go live in the woods. From there, it's all very tragic. I'm sure you'll hear the story if you stick around town.

"They 'homesteaded' somewhere up there." Lani pointed her chin toward the thick stand of fir, pine, and cedar trees creeping toward the edge of the continent, taking back what was once theirs. Cooper Springs worked hard to keep from being swallowed by the forest, but it wouldn't take much to lose the battle. "Forrest and I were both born up there. He doesn't talk about it."

"And? What happened?"

Her mouth quirked again.

"They lived in the Deep. Do you know that term?"

"No."

It sounded fucking creepy though.

"It's the central-most part of the forest that's basically untouched by humans. Obviously, my parents touched it, but you get what I mean. Legend has it that the true Deep is silent, that birds don't even live there. There's no one else."

Light rain began to mist over the windshield, and Lani flicked on the wipers. The repetitive thunk and swish was somehow comforting. Dante spotted a young mom piling her children into a minivan. One of them stood defiantly on the sidewalk with his face raised to the sky and a big smile on his face. At least one person in town enjoyed the weather.

"An especially adventurous hiker stumbled upon their outpost. I guess that's the right word. I imagine he, or she, was shocked to find a White couple and two children living up there. The hiker came back into town and reported the situation to the CSPD. Because we're a small town, the police talked to our grandfather before taking action. Like I said, I don't remember much of that time, but Forrest does. He was seven or so when our grandfather brought us to live with him."

"What happened to your parents?"

Lani shrugged. "Maybe they're still up there? I think they're dead though. Something tells me they had a suicide pact or something dramatic like that. I'm not trying to gloss over anything that happened up there—I just really don't remember it. I've been told we were undernourished, and Forrest says his first memory here in town was the heat in Grandpa's house. Of being warm and taking his first bath in a tub filled with hot water."

"You've never been curious? Never tried to find where you'd lived?"

Lani shook her head. The car slowed and she pulled to the curb in front of Dante's rental. They both looked toward the shabby house.

"The Deep isn't something to mess with. This was the mid-1980s, and there were few resources for families, especially out here in the boonies." She put the car in Park. "Shall we look around now that it's light? Maybe we'll find a carelessly forgotten business card or the perfect fingerprint."

The conversation had been effectively ended, and Dante understood. His family history was riddled with crap he'd packed away and planned never to think about again.

They didn't find anything remarkable at the rental. No abandoned car—the Honda had been towed away—no convenient clues left behind. But the murky daylight did expose sloppy footprints around the property and under the windows, along with scratch marks on the door handle where they'd tried to get inside.

They returned to the cruiser but before getting inside again, Dante glanced up and down the quiet residential street.

"Where would he go? André said he took off, jumped a fence, and was gone."

"More houses that direction." Lani gestured to the east. "And a bit further on, the edge of forest land. There's a trail that leads around it to the high school. No one reported a prowler, but let's drive over that way."

Lani took a route Dante wasn't familiar with, passing by Cooper Mansion before heading southeast along a road between the last of the houses and the trees.

"What's up with the mansion?" he asked.

At one point, the structure had been majestic, a masterpiece of Victorian architecture, but it had long ago fallen into disrepair. Windows were broken, shutters sagged. It looked like something out of a horror movie.

"Oh," Lani said airily, "just another reminder of our not-so-illustrious past. Grandfather donated it to the town as soon as he had possession. There've been all sorts of plans for the place, but they always fall through. I heard there's new grant money available, so maybe the city can finally bring it up to code. I mean, I guess it was nice to donate it, but with the amount of work it needs, it was a fairly empty gesture."

"Is it haunted too?"

Lani snickered. "I guess you'll have to stay overnight there and find out."

"Nah, I'm good."

They rounded a corner and abruptly Dante knew exactly where they were. He and André had driven this block earlier that morning.

"Deputy Trent lives down that block."

"Yep." Lani nodded. "He does. With all those creepy gnomes too."

"How easy would it be for a person to get from my street to Trent's by cutting through?"

"Pretty easy if you were fit and fast. Lots of folks around here have dogs though."

"It was pouring last night. I would think dogs would be inside, or in kennels anyway."

She waggled her head knowingly. "Most likely."

True, there were people who left their dogs out in all weather, day or night. Bastards.

"But Trent's sister said she hadn't talked to him in a few days."

"His sister? Last I knew, she was living in Chehalis. But Trent and I aren't close, so what do I know?"

"Would you be willing to stop by and talk to her? Since we're in the neighborhood. Maybe she'll tell you something that she wouldn't tell André?"

"Sure, why not?"

Dante waited in the car this time. Just like earlier, it took several moments for the sister to come to the door. While Lani spoke with her, Dante focused on the sister's body language. Was she hiding something or just uncomfortable with the cops stopping by twice in less than an hour while still in her pjs? He wasn't sure.

"Well?" he asked when Lani slipped back behind the steering wheel.

"She basically told me the same thing she told you. Hasn't spoken to Trent in a day or so."

Lani started the engine and they pulled away from the curb. Dante looked back at the house. A slat in one of the blinds was askew, as if someone had tugged on it so they could see out. She could be curious, or she could be hiding something.

They spent another forty minutes driving up and down most of the streets of Cooper Springs and not seeing anything suspicious.

"This isn't getting us anywhere, but I needed to do something," Lani said. "Let's head back to the station."

This right here was the main reason Dante was DEA and not a cop. Investigative work was often boring. He liked the thrill of being on the inside, working undercover, making things happen. He didn't have the patience for paperwork or sitting for hours at a computer.

"Let's check in at the forest services office first. The forensic anthropologist and his team are planning on heading up Crook's Trail today. We might have missed them already, but if not, I want to tell them in person to be extra careful out there. Critter thinks he's indestructible and Mags isn't much better."

"Do you think it's possible our perp hid out in the woods the rest of the night?" Dante wanted to know.

"Anything is possible. But I wouldn't want to be them. Still, I need to let Critter and Mags know there's a perp on the run."

NINETEEN

André

Carol poked her head around André's open office door. "We have a call."

Something in Carol's voice had him looking up at her sharply and immediately rising to his feet. He pulled on the damn Kevlar *again* and threw his CSPD slicker on over it. The painful call with the mayor had only just ended. He'd rather have a root canal or two than have to go through that conversation again.

Mayor Moore seemed to have a limit when it came to murder and mayhem—who knew?

"What is it?" he asked, stepping around his desk.

"Rufus Ferguson." The stricken expression on his face had her quickly adding, "That was Rufus on the phone. He went out to check on his containers and found something. A body. He says you need to come."

Damn, *another* body in a town of less than five thousand in a county of less than eighteen thousand residents? Something funky was in the water.

"When it rains, it pours," he said grimly.

"When it rains, Chief, it floods," Carol corrected.

He didn't want to leave the station, but he had to. For one, not responding wasn't an option. For two, the last thing they needed was curious town folk getting wind of yet another body and tromping all over the scene.

"Keep the doors locked while I'm gone," he instructed. "Don't let anyone inside. Radio Lani and let her know the situation."

Carol knew why Dani was hiding out in the station. Probably Morrison had told her, but Dante and André had also shared the Cliffs Notes. Were those a thing of the past?

"You can count on me, Chief Dear." Carol was unsmiling and her lips pressed together. No one was getting past her, and Dani was safer at the station than anywhere else in Cooper Springs. He hoped Morrison's Trojan horse idea worked and that they had a little breathing room to figure out what *the fuck* was going on. Unfortunately, a niggling sensation in his stomach that he'd learned to listen to over the years had him worried.

Outside, André realized Deputy Cooper was on patrol with Dante in the station's only available cruiser. Backtracking, he pushed through the back door and grabbed the keys to his Jeep. Then he headed to the location Carol had given him.

Anyone who didn't know better might think the three shipping containers were abandoned. André certainly had thought so when he first moved to town. They squatted at the back of a vacant lot owned by Rufus and not far from The Steam Donkey. André knew that, among other paraphernalia, Rufus stored various props and materials for the Shakespeare plays his son Magnus was going to put on in August.

Parking next to a sporty orange Ford Fiesta ST, André cut the engine and climbed out. What Rufus Ferguson needed with what was basically a racing car André had never asked. Waving, Rufus got out and came around to meet André at the front of his car.

"Good morning." Rufus was ensconced in a weatherproof parka, his hands tucked into the pockets.

"I suppose," André replied, not sure the morning was good at all. He, Dante, and Daniella were still alive. That was a win, he supposed. "It's been a busy one already."

"I have the feeling it's about to get busier. It's over here. I peeked just to make sure it wasn't my imagination, then called you right away."

As he spoke, Rufus led André around the three containers. Behind and partially underneath the middle one lay a blue tarp. It had been rolled into a tube and at one end André saw a pair of leather shoes, possibly boots. André thought he recognized the footwear. The soles were thick and heavy, very similar to the shoes André and Lani wore.

"Crap."

"That's what I thought."

Looking up, André took in the three containers. Two of them were a dirty shade of gray and the other was dark green.

"What brought you out here today?"

"Checking in. Magnus has some of his props stored in one—he's working on the summer production already. I have a wireless security thingy set up. Technology is pretty damn fancy these days."

He pointed upward and André saw a little round security camera mounted on the corner of one of the containers.

"I got sick of kids and or assholes spray-painting and trying to break in for shits and giggles. Got a notification last night that there was movement around them. It was raining like a horse taking a long piss at the time, so I decided to take the loss and come out when the weather calmed down."

Horse pissing was a new one. André filed it away for future use.

"Did you notice anything unusual when you arrived?"

"Other than a body wrapped in a tarp? No."

"Did you touch anything other than the edge of the tarp?"

Rufus shot him a scandalized look. "Hell no. I've watched enough TV to know better."

"I suppose I should take a look." André didn't intend to sound put upon. Whoever it was hadn't wrapped themselves in the most ubiquitous tarp on the West Coast—possibly the country—and left themselves there. Plus, he had a sinking feeling he might know who they were going to find. There was a reason Trent hadn't been answering his calls.

Pulling on a pair of plastic gloves, André crouched down to grasp the edge of the non-shoe end of the tarp. He pulled at it until he could see the victim's head clearly. What was left of it anyway.

Someone had shot Lionel Trent point-blank from close range. He'd never been a handsome man and the gunshot hadn't done him any favors. There wasn't much left of the back of his head, but his face was undamaged enough for an ID.

"Lionel Trent?" Rufus asked. "Looks like him."

André nodded and rose to his feet. "It appears so. I need to call Deputy Cooper in."

Tapping his radio, he called Lani.

"Deputy Cooper," Lani said when she picked up.

"I'm with Rufus at his er-storage lot and we've discovered a DB."

"We'll be right there."

Dante wasn't a crime scene investigator, but it would be good to have a third pair of eyes.

"I never liked Trent," Rufus said quietly. "But I didn't wish harm on him." He shrugged and met André's gaze again. "I maybe wished he'd move to Florida, so I never had to lay eyes on him again, but never this."

André wouldn't be surprised if that was how most people in

town felt about Trent. He wondered what the sister's reaction was going to be. He hadn't wanted Trent on the force but, like Rufus, André hadn't wished him bodily harm.

"We'll drop by and take your statement. There's no need to hang out in this weather. Please don't say anything because we still need to notify family."

Taking the hint, Rufus got back into his car and drove off. André had little hope that Trent's death could be kept a secret. Likely a good number of townspeople already knew André had been called out—even if he wasn't driving an official vehicle.

After taking a few pictures of the tarp and the exposed bits of Trent, André made another call and then leaned back against his Jeep. The storm turned the volume to eleven and the rain began falling like what? An elephant pissing? He tugged the slicker's hood over his head and shoved his hands into his pockets, preparing himself to wait the three minutes it would take for Lani and Dante to arrive with the evidence kit in the truck of the cruiser.

Lani stared down at the corpse while Dante came around to stand next to André.

"Damn," Lani said.

"My thoughts exactly," agreed André. "I've already called the coroner's office. George will be here as soon as he can."

"I don't like this," Dante said.

Aside from lifting the tarp, André had not moved the body. "He wasn't killed here," he said.

"Are you sure, with the way it's been raining?" Lani wondered.

"Not enough blood on the inside of the tarp," André said. "He was killed somewhere else and dumped here. Was he dumped here for us to find, or was it chance? We may have lucked out with Rufus having eyes on the property."

Instinctively, André glanced around again. Was it his imagination? He felt like they were being watched. His neck and the middle of his back had a phantom itch. Likely, it was the residents of the neighborhood wondering what was going on.

"Cooper, you canvas the neighborhood. Knock on all the houses we can see from here. Maybe somebody saw something."

"Yes, sir." Lani strode off toward the closest house, ready to knock on doors and take names.

Their eyes were on Lani as she started toward the first row of houses, so they both witnessed it when she stumbled, lurched forward, and reached for her leg before falling to the ground in a heap.

"Lani! Deputy Cooper!" André yelled, running toward his deputy.

"André!" Dante bellowed. "Over there! The shot came from over there!"

He glanced over his shoulder. Dante was pointing toward the roof of a two-story home about three hundred feet away from where Lani lay.

Squinting against the damn rain, André spotted an open window on the second story. A figure moved in the shadows, but he didn't see a weapon. The shooter was waiting to take another shot, he wasn't getting the hell out of Dodge yet. There was no help on the way, the totality of the Cooper Springs Police Department being dead, shot, or about to be shot.

Without considering that he was moving closer to danger, André continued running in a jagged line to where his fallen deputy lay, kneeling in the wet grass beside her.

"Call emergency direct!" he yelled as he unceremoniously began to drag Lani under the cover of a stand of nearby cedar trees. She would certainly die if they didn't get to safety. The ground next to him splattered as the shooter tried again. André kept moving until they were underneath a massive cedar tree.

"God dammit, André," Dante shouted. "What the fuck are you doing?"

It was perfectly obvious what he was doing so he didn't answer. André felt along Lani's neck for a pulse. She had one and it was steady. Her eyes blinked open.

"Motherfucker, that hurts," she whispered.

Lani tried to help him move her a little further, but the bullet had hit her in the thigh. Seconds later, they were around the backside of the dripping tree. André couldn't see the house clearly, which meant the shooter couldn't see him either.

Sucking in a deep breath, André had readied himself to check the extent of Lani's injury when there was another pop, like a firecracker going off, and then Dante was under the tree with them.

"I'm going to climb up and see if I can spot the fucker," he said before André could open his mouth. "I used to be a champion tree-climber. Won the under-tens in my old hood."

Dante jumped and deftly caught the lowest branch, levering himself upward. He looked back at André and Lani.

"I'll be right back."

André refocused his attention on Lani.

"Where?"

"Above my knee. Hurts fucking everywhere though."

As gently as possible, and all while listening for the sound of running footsteps or another gunshot, André ran his hand along Lani's leg to find the entry wound.

"It's bleeding but not pumping, so that's good. We need to wrap it."

With a sigh, he stripped off his slicker, the sweatshirt, and the t-shirt. Shivering, he quickly pulled his sweatshirt back on before wrapping the t-shirt around Lani's thigh. Picking up the slicker, he lay it over her like a blanket.

"It's not a tourniquet, but it'll hold until we get you to the ER."

"Why now?" Lani asked, forcing the words out. Her face was pale from the pain and blood loss.

André frowned. "What do you mean?"

"I don't see anyone through that window," Dante called down to them.

"There was someone there. I saw a shadow," he said.

"Why shoot at *me* now?" Lani whispered. "You're stuck here with me. Dante is literally up a tree. Dani is alone at the station with Carol."

"I told Carol to keep all the doors locked."

But an even worse feeling started to creep up his spine—the one in his stomach was already working overtime.

"Fuck."

Lani was right; they'd been effectively separated. Who would break into a police station? The same psychotic motherfucker who'd taken two shots at André, tried to get into Dante's house, and murdered Lionel Trent, that's who. Someone extremely dangerous.

"Dante, get your ass down here. One of us needs to get back to the station."

"Both of you go, sir." Lani tried to sit up again, gritting her teeth against the pain. "I'll be fine."

"One of us needs to stay with you."

"I don't think so. Whoever it was is gone now. I think they need both of you at the station."

Dante crashed to the ground next to them as if he'd leaped out of the tree instead of climbing back down. André glanced around, willing a solution to occur to him that didn't involve leaving Lani on her own. He wasn't about to ask a resident to risk their life, even if he suspected that Lani was right, and the shooter was gone. With Trent dead and Lani out of commission, CSPD was down to one person.

Him.

"I have my weapon, sir. Lean me up against the trunk of the tree, like Clint Eastwood. I'll be good."

Abruptly, an orange Ford Fiesta came racing down the street

and stopped on the wrong side, close to where the three of them were huddled.

Rufus rolled the driver's side window down.

"Get her in."

André briefly debated arguing with the older man, to order him to get away from an active crime scene. But what good would it do them? Lani needed to get to the ER. André and Dante had to get back to the station.

"Can you get Lani to the ER?" he asked. "Dante and I have something we need to take care of."

Rufus lifted his hand to his forehead in a makeshift salute. "Glad to be of service. Load her up."

Ignoring the little voice in his head asking him if it was proper procedure to ask this of an older civilian, he and Dante lifted Lani off the ground. In under a minute, she was wrapped in a spare blanket and strapped into the back of the Fiesta. All without any more gunshots—Lani and Dante were right, the shooter was gone. Rufus took off, heading south toward Aberdeen, and André and Dante didn't hesitate.

"I need to clear the house," André said. "Take my Jeep and get back to the station."

"Fuck that, we'll call and tell them to lock up tight. I'm not letting you go inside that house alone."

There was no time to argue. Ignoring him, André jogged across the roadway to the house in question. A neighbor ventured out onto their porch.

"Get inside," André ordered. "This is a police matter."

"The house is a vacation rental. Several men have been staying there a few days now," the man yelled before scurrying back inside.

"Several men? Surely if one of them had been Deputy Trent, that guy would have said so?" Dante observed.

They mounted the porch stairs. André was already second-guessing himself. Maybe they should have immediately returned to the station. But there was immediate danger right here and it was literally his job to protect the residents of Cooper Springs. Carol had locked all the doors in the station. She and Dani would be fine.

And there was a bridge for sale too.

With Dante by his side, André rapped on the door. There was no answer, not that he had expected one.

"Again?" prompted Dante. "Or should one of us go around back?"

Shaking his head, André banged on the door again, louder and longer. This time he thought he heard a sound. Something anyway.

"Did you hear that?"

"Maybe," André said. "It could have been the wind."

"This is ridiculous." Dante grasped the door handle and twisted it. To both their surprise, it turned. Glancing at André, Dante turned the handle as far as it would go, pushing the door open as he did so.

It opened into a bland—and empty—living room. The laminate floor was covered by an area rug and a sectional couch took up one corner. On a nice day, visitors would look out on the backside of the cliff. In front of the couch was a coffee table with an oversize book of the history of the area and a three-ring binder labeled *Information* displayed on it. André noted the binder was only a half-inch thick.

Something that sounded like a moan came from the next room. André and Dante glanced at each other and nodded. Splitting up so André could take one side of the archway and Dante the other, they moved closer.

They hadn't needed to be stealthy. Just inside the kitchen lay a man in a pool of blood. His own, presumably, since he was bleeding from his gut and had his hands pressed against the wound in a futile attempt to stop the flow.

"Mike Jensen," André stated.

"The fuck? It is Jensen," Dante exclaimed. He dropped to his knees next to the man and pulled his hands away from the bloody mess. What he saw wasn't pretty and André had to force himself to look at it. The wound looked mortal to him, but he wasn't a surgeon.

Spinning around, he jerked drawers open until he found a stack of kitchen towels. Kneeling on Jensen's other side, André stacked the towels together and pressed them against the wound. They quickly turned crimson.

"How do you know Jensen?" Dante asked.

"He was my partner on the Campos apprehension team."

They stared at each other and then at Jensen, both drawing a similar conclusion. Jensen was the leak.

"Jensen, who shot you? What the fuck happened here?" André had his phone out again and was already on the line, requesting an emergency airlift. He worried the air ambulance would not arrive in time, but he had to try. He glanced out the nearest window; at least it wasn't raining sideways anymore.

Jensen lifted his lids halfway, and his lips moved. Whatever he said, André couldn't quite hear him. Or he couldn't believe what he was hearing. He glanced down at Dante, whose head was cocked so he could listen closely.

"*What* is he saying?"

Dante looked back up at André, his eyes wide. "Campos, he said *Campos*."

"Alonso Campos? Alonso Campos shot Jensen?" André almost couldn't believe what he was hearing.

Jensen moved his head up and down infinitesimally.

"The fuck? What the fuck did you do? Did you bring him here? You were working with that scum?" And yet the man outside had said that two men were staying in the house.

Jensen had known André moved to Cooper Springs; he'd been at the going-away party. André's new location wasn't a secret. But

Dante arriving with Dani must've been a bonus. And if he was on the take—

"Money... need to go," he whispered, "after the girl. You... next. I... thought I was smart." His head lolled to the side.

Dante and André stared at each other.

From a distance came the whomp-whomp sound of helicopter blades.

Ten minutes later, they watched as Jensen was loaded into the copter. The pilot gave him the thumbs-up, and they lifted off again. André didn't believe in a god, but Jensen was going to need a miracle and André wasn't sure he deserved one.

They left André's Jeep behind, and he drove the cruiser. Next to him, Dante called the station for the third time. For the third time, he set his cell phone in his lap and stared out the windshield.

The only thing to do was set a land-speed record to the other end of town.

They had allowed themselves to be lured away from the one person they were supposed to be protecting. And now, Carol—who was supposed to be retiring and living her best life, traveling the United States in an RV with her husband of thirty-five years—wasn't answering their calls.

They were being drawn into a trap and they both knew it. There was nowhere else to go. Alonso Campos planned on killing them all. Of that, André had no doubt.

André jammed the gas pedal all the way to the floor, and the cruiser lurched forward. Damn, he hoped they had one working cruiser after this was over. Because it was going to be over, and they were all going to survive. He couldn't allow himself to imagine any other outcome. This bullshit was coming to an end. Whoever'd killed Deputy Trent, injured Deputy Cooper, murdered Simone Maddison, and tried to kill Dante—André'd had fucking enough.

He wasn't planning on taking prisoners.

"This is absolutely Campos's work," André said as they careened around the last corner and the station was in view. "This has nothing to do with your brother. I don't know why Alonso would kill Trent, but we'll cross that road later. The fact that you and I specifically have been targeted is the key, and Jensen just pretty much confirmed that. I bet Trent was feeding Campos information about me and Jensen was—what the fuck was he thinking?"

"He was thinking he was smarter than Alonso," Dante said. "Probably thought he could control him. But Alonso is a snake. The only person he listens to is his brother, and Aldo is out of reach."

"What a fucking idiot. I never did like working with him. We brought big brother in, Jensen and me. But his crazy-ass younger brother was in the wind. And there wasn't enough evidence to go after him at the time. We all knew Alonso was involved, but Aldo kept him off the books. Now I'm wondering if Jensen had something to do with that too."

"I agree. Jensen always has been a cocky bastard. Alonso's going down this time, no fucking mercy."

There wasn't time to make a plan—taking more time meant lives. He refused to let himself think that they'd already wasted too much of it.

André gave up trying to radio the station. Instead, he put a belated officer-down call into the Grays County Sheriff's Office, then pulled the car over about half a block before the station. He'd already broken so many rules that he didn't think another few were going to matter.

"He knows we're coming," André said through clenched teeth. "We might as well try and surprise him. With Woods and Jensen out of the picture, there's two of us and one of him."

"We hope there's only one," Dante said over the top of the car after they got out.

André nodded. One would be much better odds.

"We'll cut around the auto shop and come in behind the station. I'll take the back door and you go around the side to take the front entrance. As far as I know, there aren't any convenient air-conditioning vents to climb in through. We're just going to have to get inside without getting dead."

"I don't feel great about splitting up."

"It's all we've got. When we get there, stick to the side of the building."

"You think I was born yesterday?"

"Just... no."

Grabbing Dante by the collar of his jacket, André pulled him close.

"Don't you dare die on me."

Fleetingly, he pressed his lips against Dante's before stepping away and disappearing around the side of the auto shop without looking back. Once a marshal, always a marshal.

TWENTY

Dante

André vanished through the bushes into the parking lot before Dante could tell him he loved him and to be careful. Neither one of them were going to be careful. It wasn't in their natures. And by this point Dante hoped André knew he was damn serious about him.

Swiftly, he adjusted his ballistic vest and made sure his holster was unsnapped. Then Dante made his way along the front of the auto shop, hoping he was staying away from any fucking cameras. The last thing they needed was the owner calling the cops. As soon as he had the thought, he snorted.

There were no cops to call.

When he reached the corner, Dante halted. He took in the quiet, serene-appearing police building and the area around it. With the storm raging, no pedestrians were making their way along the sidewalk. Thank fuck. No beachcombers were coming in or heading out to the mile-long stretch of sandy beach across the way. It felt desolate. Deserted. Almost a ghost town.

Steeling himself for what he might find, Dante started toward the front door of the station. This exposed him to anyone who might happen to be driving down the street, but it was the only choice. As he stepped closer, staying as close to the wall as possible, his cell phone vibrated. Only three people knew this number and one of them was Dani. Had the text been trapped in cellular purgatory until now? Or was she texting at this moment? Was it Chris Hatch? He knew it wasn't André.

He paused again, his back pressed against the cement wall of the station, and pulled his cellphone out of his pocket.

Dani: There's someone here.

He swore violently under his breath.

When the message had been sent, Dani had been alive. Dante was going to hold on to the hope she still was, that the text had been from seconds, not minutes, ago. He didn't reply. There was no reason to alert The Motherfucker that one of them had a phone. Instead, he jammed it back into his pocket and continued toward the front entrance.

I'll be right there, little mouse. I'll be right there.

The front door was ajar, moving ever so slightly back and forth every time the wind found its way into the alcove. Dante tried to see inside, but the lobby lights appeared to have been turned off. Over the wind and rain, Dante could hear nothing but the beating of his heart.

Grabbing his weapon, he held it up and out loosely with both hands, something he'd practiced so often he could do it sleepwalking.

"Now or never," he murmured. "We're coming for you, Alonso."

Springing forward, Dante crashed into the door shoulder-first, using his body weight to propel him inside the building. In a half-crouch, he scanned the room, his weapon still at the ready. Carol's computer had been swept to the floor where it lay in a heap, the screen cracked and the keyboard smashed. The desk calendar and Rolodex had met a similar fate. Neither Carol nor Dani were in sight. That was good.

But where were they?

The only way to find out was to choose a corridor, right or left, and hope he guessed correctly.

Fifty years ago, the building had been constructed in a semi-shotgun style, which meant that when Dante inched over and peered down the hallway where the holding cells and André's office were, he could see all the way to the back door. The evidence room and armory were off the other hallway.

If he were a betting man, or a woman who'd worked the front desk for years and had a young adult to protect, where would he hide? Dani had been in the breakroom. If Carol had any warning, Dante suspected instinct would propel her to get to Dani. Carol knew the station better than anyone, including André. Where the fuck were they?

"All clear," André said quietly, emerging from the hallway on the right and looking around the lobby. "Crap, this doesn't look good."

"Campos." Dante gave up being patient. "We know it's you. Quit terrorizing an old woman and teen girl and fight like a man."

During his years in law enforcement, one thing Dante knew for sure was that men like Alonso Campos had a knee-jerk reaction to being called not a man. Dante had his theories about that, but they didn't matter. Campos was certifiable.

There was no reply, just the wind prowling its way inside and creating a mini whirlwind with Carol's paperwork. Dante and André glanced at each other.

"Behind me," André ordered in a barely audible murmur.

As much as Dante wanted to take the lead, because Dani was somewhere in the building, he nodded.

"The hallway is clear," André whispered as he kept moving. "Checking the breakroom."

The sound of a door slamming against a wall was followed by silence. Dante crept down the corridor in André's wake. The breakroom was empty too. Playing cards had fallen to the floor and that was the only sign of Dani.

From the next room came a muffled crashing sound. Dante froze. Had Alonso gotten into the armory? Surely it was secured at all times.

"Fuck," muttered André. "That room should be locked."

"Pretty sure all sorts of rules are being broken around here today."

They swung around, each taking one side of the door.

"Police! Come out with your hands over your head," André yelled.

There were some shuffling noises on the other side of the door.

"Just a moment, sir," Carol called out.

Dante felt lightheaded at the sound of the older woman's voice, and he moved around to stand at André's side. More shuffling sounds ensued before the door opened a crack. A narrow strip of Carol was visible.

"Oh, excellent, it is you, sir. I just wanted to make sure this dirtbag didn't have any friends on the way. He kept talking about his brother."

Carol pulled the door open wider. On the floor of the small room was the body of a man—Alonso Campos, Dante was reasonably sure. He looked down to see a Springfield pistol held firmly in Carol's left hand. Dani was crouched in the corner behind her.

"I'm a southpaw," she said with a shrug. "Always did give me an advantage."

Dante and André's attention returned to the body that lay crumpled on the floor. Carol's gaze followed theirs.

"What happened?" asked André.

"As part of my job, I keep the weapons stored here clean and ready. I was a damn good shot in my day too. This man"—she nudged a leg with her toe—"made it easy for me though. He didn't expect a little old lady to fight back."

Dani ran to Dante, and he wrapped his arms around his niece, hugging her to him.

"I'm sorry I wasn't here, topolina."

"It's okay—he's dead now."

"Tell us what happened."

"I was playing cards and Carol came back and told me to hide in here. She saw him on a camera in the back, I guess."

Carol nodded, setting the weapon down on the worktable. "Yep, saw the bastard as bold as day."

"Then we waited for him to find us. He opened the door and before he could shoot us, Carol shot him. Actually," Dani said with a grin, "Luna bit him in the leg and then Carol shot him."

Luna, who'd been sitting quietly in a corner, perked up at the sound of her name.

"Good girl," said Dante, patting the top of the dog's head. "Very good girl. Extra treats for life."

"I didn't think a stranger sneaking into the station carrying a hunting rifle was up to any good," Carol explained. "All I had to do was look in his eyes for one second, and I knew he was pure evil."

"It was my fault he got in. I took Luna out to pee in the parking lot and forgot to lock the door when we came back in," Dani said, a guilty expression on her face.

"Don't even think about blaming yourself," Dante assured her. "Alonso Campos was determined to find you. He would have gotten in here regardless. And maybe it was better that it was easy. He didn't expect anyone to fight back. He thought he would just waltz in."

They all froze when a deep voice called out, "Grays County sheriff! Stay where you are!"

. . .

Between the murder of Lionel Trent and the timely death of Alonso Campos, it was far into the night before André and Dante were alone together. Dani and Carol had been questioned, and once they were given the all clear, Carol had taken Dani to her house.

"Luna can come along, and I'll figure out something to make for dinner. You can help if you like. Or maybe Marcus will cook," she'd added. "We've had a long day."

"I'll be there as soon as I can," Dante assured his niece.

A couple of hours into the circus, Morrison and Hatch arrived together. By that time, Rufus had already called in with an update on Lani Cooper. She would make a full recovery, although she'd needed surgery to remove the bullet and repair a damaged ligament.

"Sounds like she'll be on desk duty for a while, Chief. Forrest is her with her now," Rufus said. "I'm gonna head home. It's been a damn long day."

Lionel Trent's body was officially ID'd by his sister, who, in fact, had been living at Trent's house for a few weeks. Once they began questioning her, they learned that Deputy Trent had been acting secretive and meeting up with someone, but he'd never told her who it was, just saying he was doing some work that would change Cooper Springs. Since her brother always had one or two get-rich schemes going, she didn't inquire further. Then, two nights ago, a stranger had shown up at the door and demanded to be let inside.

"I didn't like him and told Trent so. The man said something about how he better be getting his money's worth. I asked Lionel what he meant, and he told me to forget I ever heard anything. The next morning, Lionel left for work and that was the last time I saw him."

Dante knew Trent hadn't shown up for his shift. He'd probably already been dead by then. Maybe he'd threatened Alonso or asked for more cash. There would likely be some kind of money trail. If they could trace it to Aldo, big brother could count on more charges being added to his already long list of crimes. They didn't know for sure yet, but both André and Dante suspected Trent had been keeping Alonso aware of André's whereabouts.

Hatch nodded, taking notes while Dante recounted what Paulette Trent had told them.

"After killing Simone, Alonso Campos wanted Dani dead. He'd convinced himself that killing her would mean Aldo would go free. Which makes no sense. I'll bet he didn't expect to find Dante and Daniella living in Cooper Springs. That must have been a little bonus for him," Morrison mused. "Big brother would have been so happy had Alonso brought those trophies to him."

"And Jensen was playing both sides." Dante mused. "Was he the only one in Campos's pocket?"

"We hope so. Now that Daniella and you are out of the woods, I can breathe easier," Hatch muttered. "No need to ask again about WITSEC."

"Alonso didn't fall for the Trojan horse plan," Dante pointed out. "And with Jensen feeding him inside information, Campos could have known if we went into protection. And again, our answer would have been no."

"But he wouldn't have known where you were," André interjected. "We are very good at hiding people."

Dante frowned. Was it selfish of him to bristle at the thought of going into hiding without André?

Morrison glared at Dante. "It was a good idea," he insisted. "It's not my fault Jensen was a traitor."

"It was a fine idea," André assured the other agent, completely unaware that Dante was stewing over a scenario with no base in reality—at least, not any longer.

"See, even André here thought it was a good plan."

Hatch shot André an enigmatic look across the table. "Can we speak in your office?"

TWENTY-ONE

André

André tried his best, but he couldn't hold it back any longer. A massive yawn escaped him. The adrenaline had worn off hours ago, and the five or so cups of coffee he'd had since then were no longer pulling their weight. It was possible the coffee was actually making him sleepier.

"Am I boring you?" Christopher Hatch asked, his sharp gaze drilling into André's.

What was his problem?

"No, but it's been a day, hasn't it? I have a team in town from West Coast Forensics retrieving remains discovered earlier—" In the week? Month? André had lost track of time.

"Lizzy Harlow's murder case is growing colder by the minute. I'd like to get a few hours' sleep before taking that on in the morning. Not to mention I'm down to one officer—that's me, in case you haven't figured that out—and have a town to keep an eye on." André didn't like the DEA officer. They'd never crossed paths before, but something about him rubbed André the wrong way.

Hatch tossed down the pen he'd snagged from André's collection. "I suppose we have enough for now. If I think of anything, I'll let you know immediately. If you think of anything, call us immediately." He handed André a business card.

"Will do," André said, taking the card and touching his forehead in a mock salute.

Instead of getting up to leave, like André was willing him to, Hatch stayed where he was—behind André's desk. The room had been somewhat tidied up, but André's murder board still lay in a corner along with other paperwork he was going to have to sort through and reorganize.

"West Coast Forensics, huh? They have a good reputation."

As if the man wasn't aware that WCF was one of the best independent investigation organizations in the country.

"I'm very lucky they've agreed to help us out here in Cooper Springs. It turns out that the mayor's son is their forensic anthropologist."

André shifted in his seat, wanting to be released. It felt like the last day of school and Hatch was keeping him back just to taunt him. They all knew that, if it hadn't been for Carol's quick thinking, the outcome today could have been tragic. What was Hatch doing still asking him questions?

"You've known Castone for a while now?"

"A couple years. Close to that anyway." Where the hell was this going? Why was Hatch asking him about Dante?

"He's an interesting man. Until his sister was killed, I never saw him as the type of person to leave the agency. I just figured he was one of those who'd stay forever, die with his boots on, that kind of thing."

Hatch picked up the pen and was flipping it back and forth between his index and middle fingers before dropping it again.

"Pardon me," André said, leaning forward, "but can I ask what this has to do with what happened today or in the past weeks?"

Hatch sat back in André's chair, behind André's desk. Seeing him there was starting to piss him off.

"Nothing really. I've been Castone's handler for, needless to say, a while now. Years. I've watched him go under and come back out many times. He's a good man. A man I'm going to miss. I hope you appreciate just what kind of man he is."

André studied the DEA handler closely.

Hatch picked up the damn pen for the third time and began doodling nothings on the edges of the purloined notepad. A sideways thought occurred to André. He almost opened his mouth and asked straight out. But he didn't.

Had Hatch been interested in Dante—as more than his employee?

Hatch looked up from the paper, meeting his gaze. He saw disappointment, loss, and deep loneliness. André knew he was right.

"Take care of him," Hatch finally said. "I managed to keep him alive this long."

They took André's Jeep to pick up Daniella and the dog from Carol's house. Dante insisted on driving. André didn't care who drove or where they went as long as they were heading home. All of them, including Luna.

"Is it really over, Zio?" Dani asked from the back seat.

"We think so."

"And we know who killed Mom?"

"Yes, and he's dead too. Not ideal, but it means he can't do anything to hurt you anymore."

Dani fell silent and André's stomach growled loudly enough to be heard over the windshield wipers. The car slowed as Dante glanced over at him.

"Eyes on the road," André muttered. "I'm hungry, big f-ing deal."

"Zio likes to feed people," Dani said. "Mom used to say he was going to make a great husband someday."

"And I used to tell your mom that she was making a big assumption there."

"Huh."

André could almost hear Dani thinking.

"Mr. Barone and Mr. Stone are dating. Romy thinks they might get married someday but that Mr. Stone is afraid of commitment, so her dad is going to have to work hard to convince him."

Luckily, André's stomach rumbled again and then Dante was parking in front of André's house and all discussion of relationships and marriage was forgotten for the time being.

They all got out of the car, Luna racing to the front door to wait for the slow humans. Even after the past forty-eight hours, even hungry and exhausted, André felt himself smile. He'd never allowed himself to dream of a partner, a dog, and or a picket fence. Or a teenager. But he liked Daniella, she was a sharp kid.

He allowed his imagination to spool out a few years, envisioning sitting on a porch somewhere with Dante—not this house, it didn't have a big enough porch—and waiting for Dani to arrive for a visit from college. There was a dog somewhere in there too.

"Are you coming?" Dante asked.

EPILOGUE

André twitched his suit jacket down and ran his hand across the front of it, unable to hide his grin as he pushed open the lobby doors and stepped into the late-morning sunshine. Summer was in full force and the steel and glass United States Courthouse in Portland, Oregon, sparkled—almost as if it too was proud that the verdict had been life with no parole considerations for many, many years.

The likelihood that Aldo Campos would die from natural causes before the parole board ever saw him was nearly certain. That Jensen hadn't survived emergency surgery was another sort of justice, André supposed. He was dead and couldn't do any more damage.

He glanced around but didn't immediately see Dante.

"André, over here."

Peering into the sunshine, André spotted his favorite person. Dante Castone was occupying a table outside the coffee shop on the other side of the street. Taking a deep breath, then rolling his shoulders and checking for traffic, he made his way across the busy roadway. It was possible he sauntered.

"Well?" Dante asked, smiling up at him when he arrived.

André's grin widened further. "It's official. Aldo Campos is going away for a very long time. But you knew that."

"Yes, well, maybe I wanted to hear it from you. Makes it seem more real."

Behind André, a driver laid on their horn. A different driver yelled something obscene out their window. Really? At ten thirty in the morning? What was wrong with people?

"Are we staying or getting the hell out of here?" André was ready to leave.

After almost two years away, Portland was not André's city any longer. During the week he'd hung around waiting to be called to testify, he'd missed the ocean with its varying moods and the clouds that were either overhead or lurking just around the corner.

He'd missed the police station, even with all its quirks—including Nick Waugh. Carol had been right about him. Nick was proving to be an excellent front desk manager and dispatch officer. The two new deputies they'd hired seemed to be learning quickly, and the recovered Deputy Lani Cooper had done an excellent job filling in for André while he'd been away in Portland.

Things were good in his universe.

"Let's shake the dust of this city off our feet." Dante picked up a to-go cup from the table and handed it to him. "Hopefully, it's still warm."

Before strapping himself into the passenger seat for the ride home, André stripped off his suit jacket and tossed it in the back of Dante's car. His roller bag was already stashed there, along with what looked like a duffle bag.

"Thanks for picking my bag up. Did you bring laundry?" he teased.

"Maybe," Dante replied. "Get in already. I want to try and avoid the traffic."

. . .

Hours later, Dante finally pulled to a stop in front of what looked like a one-room cabin.

"What's this?" André asked.

"It's you and me escaping for another two nights. Alone. No teens. No dog needing to pee at four a.m. Just us."

André had to admit that sounded nice. They weren't officially living together, but André tended to stay at Dante's most of the time. After living alone for most of his adult life, André was surprised how quickly and painlessly he'd adapted to sharing space with Dante.

Xavier Stone was keeping an eye out for a house for them. The elderly owners of Pizza Mart had accepted Dante's offer to buy the restaurant. Cooper Springs would soon have an Italian café— Dante Castone style. The remodel was almost finished, with the grand opening scheduled for just two weeks from now—smack in the middle of Magnus Ferguson's Shakespeare beach theater production. Life was damn good.

"Come on, let's go inside. We have a lot to celebrate."

Dante popped open the car door and climbed out.

"Oh, good, more celebrating," teased André as Dante unlocked the door and ushered him into the tiny space. They celebrated a lot and it usually ended with them wrapped around each other in bed.

The cabin was furnished with a bed covered with a colorful quilt that looked handmade, a kitchenette, and a tiny table for eating at or possibly doing jigsaw puzzles—there were a few stacked on a built-in shelf. The bed would be getting a lot of use.

"Are you sure we have time for this, with Osteria Castone opening so soon?"

André set his roller bag next to the door while Dante began unpacking the groceries he'd stopped for a few miles back. The bottle of prosecco he left out on the counter.

"We have more time now than we will for a while. And you've

been gone. I missed you, so I'm being selfish and stealing you away for one extra night. Lani can handle it."

"I'm afraid she's going to handle me being gone so well, I'll be out of a job."

"Nah," Dante said, "she doesn't like all the paperwork."

"Nobody likes it."

"You can't fool me, André, with your abnormal love for spreadsheets."

"I do enjoy a good spreadsheet." André laughed. "And pivot tables."

"Sicko. But I love you anyway, André Dear. I'll never get tired of telling you."

Who else knew that gruff, rough Dante Castone had a hidden soft center? André suspected that the list was short: Daniella, André, and Luna. That was fine with André; he didn't want to share.

"I love you too, Dante."

Dante popped the cork out of the bottle and poured each of them a glass of the sparkling wine. He'd even brought plastic champagne glasses.

"You think of everything."

Dante smirked. "I do. I even found a couple of cozies by that new author you like."

"You did?"

André moved to set down his prosecco so he could check out the books, but Dante stopped him.

"Toast first and, you know, *other* things before I lose you to the life and crimes of the Red Nipper, or whatever you're reading at the moment."

"The Red Nipper?" André repeated. "Is that an elderly serial killer who uses fingernail clippers?"

With a smile and a shake of his head, Dante held out his glass. "To you and me finally getting it right."

"To us," André agreed, bumping his glass against Dante's.

He met Dante's warm gaze and they both took a healthy sip of the sparkling wine. Then, still looking into each other's eyes, they set the glasses down onto the small table. With a satisfied smile, Dante moved into André's space and wrapped his arms around him.

"Let's get to the next part of this celebration." His deft fingers fiddled with the top button of André's shirt and moved on to the next. "Then I will make us dinner."

André started loosening Dante's belt so he could get to the snap on his jeans.

"I won't argue with that."

"You would if you could." The words were muffled though, since Dante had finished with André's shirt and had dropped to his knees.

Later, André stretched and rolled out of the bed. It was pretty comfortable for a state park-sourced mattress. But he was more interested in the man on the other side of the room.

"I could get used to watching you cook mostly naked."

Dante's shoulders shook with silent laugher as he stirred the red sauce he was heating up for their dinner. "Unlike Morrison, I am not going to scald my junk."

"I very much appreciate your diligence."

Unzipping his roller bag, André pulled out a pair of fresh boxers, Levis, and a t-shirt. Once he wouldn't scare anyone who might stroll past their small cabin, he padded to the window and looked out over the small bay.

The swoop and rise of dark wings over the water caught his attention. What looked to be a crow flew out from the woods and across the bay, directly toward the scraggly line of vacation cottages. As it swiftly closed the distance to the cabins, André realized he was seeing a damn huge raven.

"Whoa," he murmured, stepping as close as he could to the window.

The raven slowed its wings and banked slightly. And then, with an abruptness that shocked him, it was directly in front of André, landing in a flurry of motion on the tiny, covered patio.

Not wanting to scare it away, André stayed perfectly still, hardly breathing. Beady black eyes filled with intelligence of a different kind seemed to be looking through the window right at him. He could literally feel the animal observing him, judging him.

The creature cocked its head to one side almost as if listening for something—or maybe someone? When it didn't seem to hear anything, the bird slowly lowered its head and opened its beak to let an object drop to the ground. Whatever the thing was, it landed with an audible smack against the wood decking.

Lifting its head again, the raven stared directly into the window at the spot where André stood inside. The intensity of its scrutiny was not something André would forget quickly. Then, with a flap of its huge wings, the raven took flight again, soaring back across the bay and disappearing back into the woods.

"What the fuck was that?" Dante asked from directly behind him.

"I have no idea."

Opening the door, André stepped outside, curious to see what the big bird had left behind. The thirty-second encounter had seemed so purposeful, intentional. The object sparkled in the dying summer sunshine.

Bending down, André picked up the circle of gold and examined it closely. An empty setting gaped where a tiny gem had once been safely nestled. He'd need his reading glasses for the engraving he could feel on the inside of the band.

"A ring? The crow brought you a present?"

"That was a raven," André corrected. "And, yes, oddly enough, I think it did."

∾

Don't miss The Beginning — A spooky short story involving Rufus Ferguson!

∾

Next up: Code Violation

Trust is a thing of the past. All that matters is the truth.

Forrest Cooper

Has a short list of people he trusts. His sister. Xavier Stone. Magnus and Rufus Ferguson. A nosey newcomer to Cooper Springs is not making his list. Ever.

Nero Vik

Produces a podcast about unsolved murders all over the country. He's in town following his instinct. At last, he may have found his cousin's final resting place.

Forrest is not giving the new guy an inch, much less discussing his sordid family history with him. His past, his sister's past, is not up for debate on some nickel-and-dime podcast.

Nero was the last of his family to see his cousin alive. He was the one who said, *maybe you shouldn't*. But Donny was someone who never backed down. He got into that van.

One man has dedicated himself to putting his past where it belongs—behind him. He has a lavender farm and after a lot of therapy, he sleeps at night. Most of the time.

The other is determined to expose the truth—no matter how painful it is. He's lived with crippling guilt since he was twelve. Twenty-five years later he's close to the truth and he's not backing away now.

The perfect storm brings them together. Will they make it through to the other side?

Code Violation is book four in the Reclaimed Heart series.

Stay up to date on all things Elle related by joining the Highway to Elle. A weekly newsletter with all the Elle news you'll ever need!

A THANK YOU FROM ELLE

If you enjoyed *Red Flagged*, I would greatly appreciate if you would let your friends know so they can experience André, Dante, and the rest of Cooper Springs As with all of my books, I have enabled lending on all platforms in which it is allowed to make it easy to share with a friend. If you leave a review for Red Flagged or any of my books, on the site from which you purchased the book, Goodreads, Bookbub, or your own blog, I would love to read it! Email me the link at elle@ellekeaton.com

Keep up-to-date with new releases and sales, *The Highway to Elle* hits your in-box approximately every two weeks, sometimes more sometimes less. I include deals, freebies and new releases as well as a sort of rambling running commentary on what *this* author's life is like. I'd love to have you aboard! I also have a reader group called the Highway to Elle, come say hi!

ABOUT ELLE

Writing inclusive romance featuring complex characters and a unique sense of place is my happy place. The characters start out broken, and maybe they're still a tad banged up by the end, but they do find the other half of their hearts and ALWAYS get their happily ever after.

In 2017 I pressed the publish button for the first time and never looked back—making this the longest period of time I've stuck with a job--in my entire life. Currently, there are over thirty Elle Keaton books available for you to read or listen to.

I love cats and dogs. Star Wars and Star Trek. Pineapple on pizza, and have a cribbage habit my husband encourages. Connecting with readers is very important to me. If you are so inclined, join my newsletter, The Highway to Elle, and keep up to date with everything Elle related.

Including, but not limited to, 'where are my glasses?', and 'why are there cats?'. I can also be found on Facebook, Instagram and occasionally TikTok.

Cover designed by: Tiffany Black

Edited by: The Elusive SB

Cover Photo: CJC Photography

Cover Model: Zachary Vazquez